D0971198

DISNEY

ZOOTOPIA

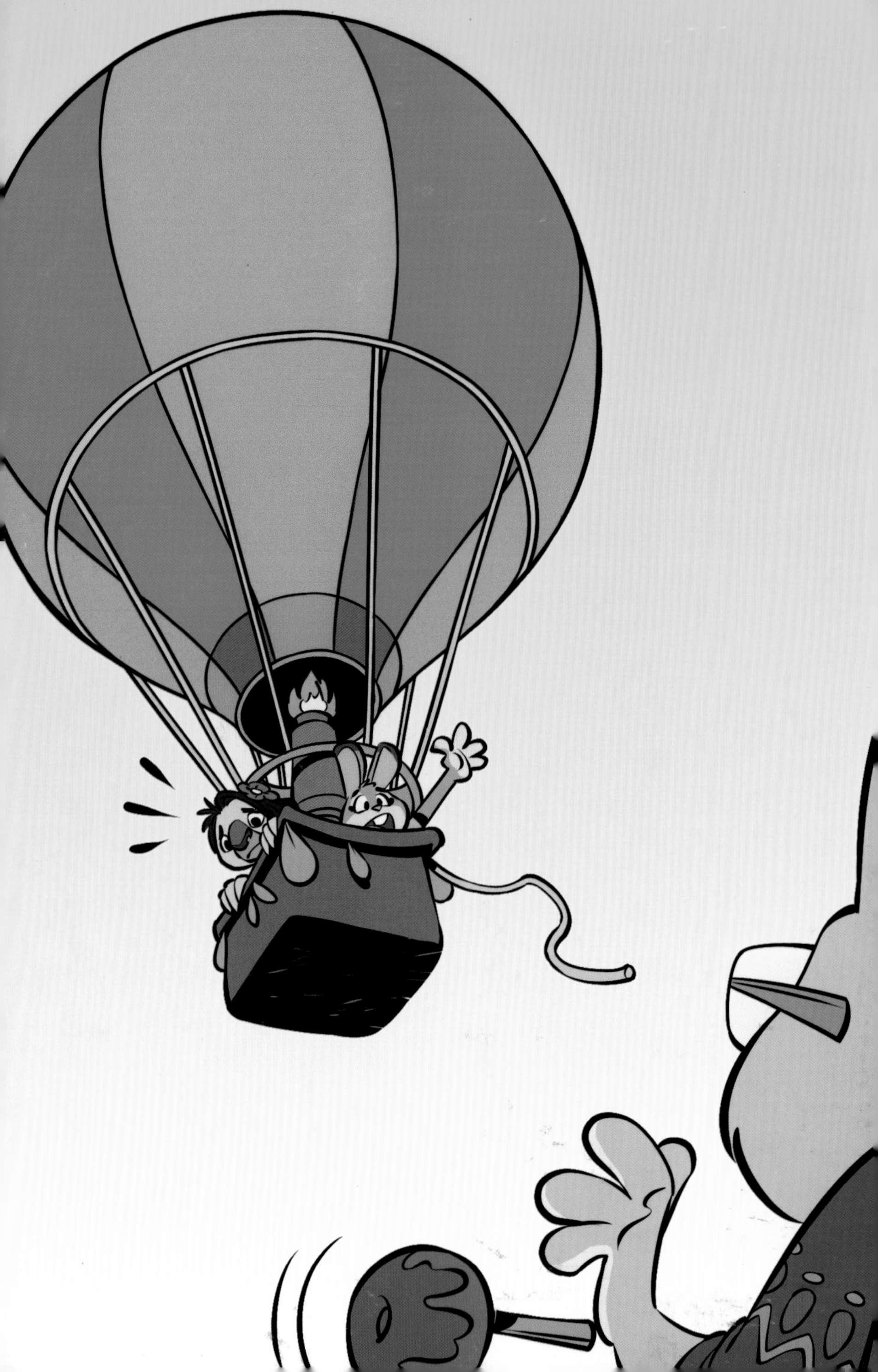

DISNEY
ZOOTOPIA

FRIENDS TO THE RESCUE

Script by
Jimmy Gownley

Art by
Leandro Ricardo da Silva

Colors by
Wes Dzioba

Lettering by
Chris Dickey

Dark Horse Books

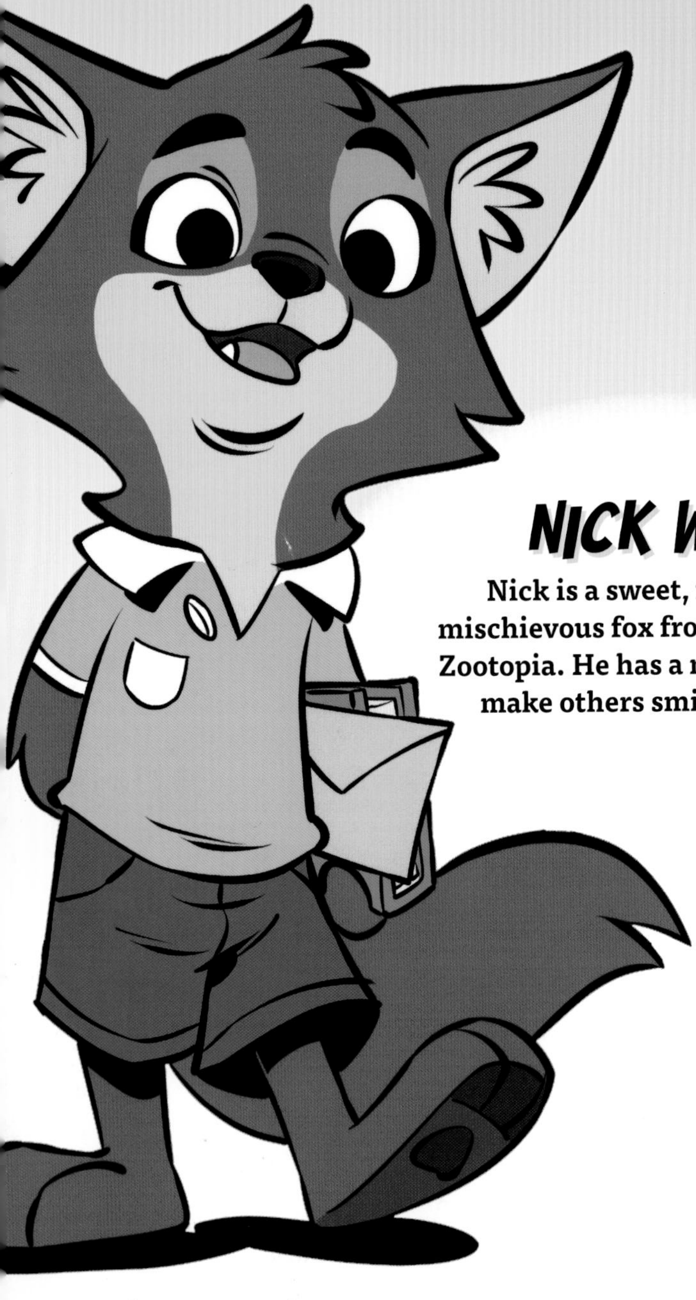

NICK WILDE

Nick is a sweet, friendly, and mischievous fox from the big city of Zootopia. He has a natural ability to make others smile and laugh.

JUDY HOPPS

Judy is an energetic, clever, and big-hearted bunny from the rural town of Bunnyburrow. She loves helping others and will lend a paw at any chance she gets.

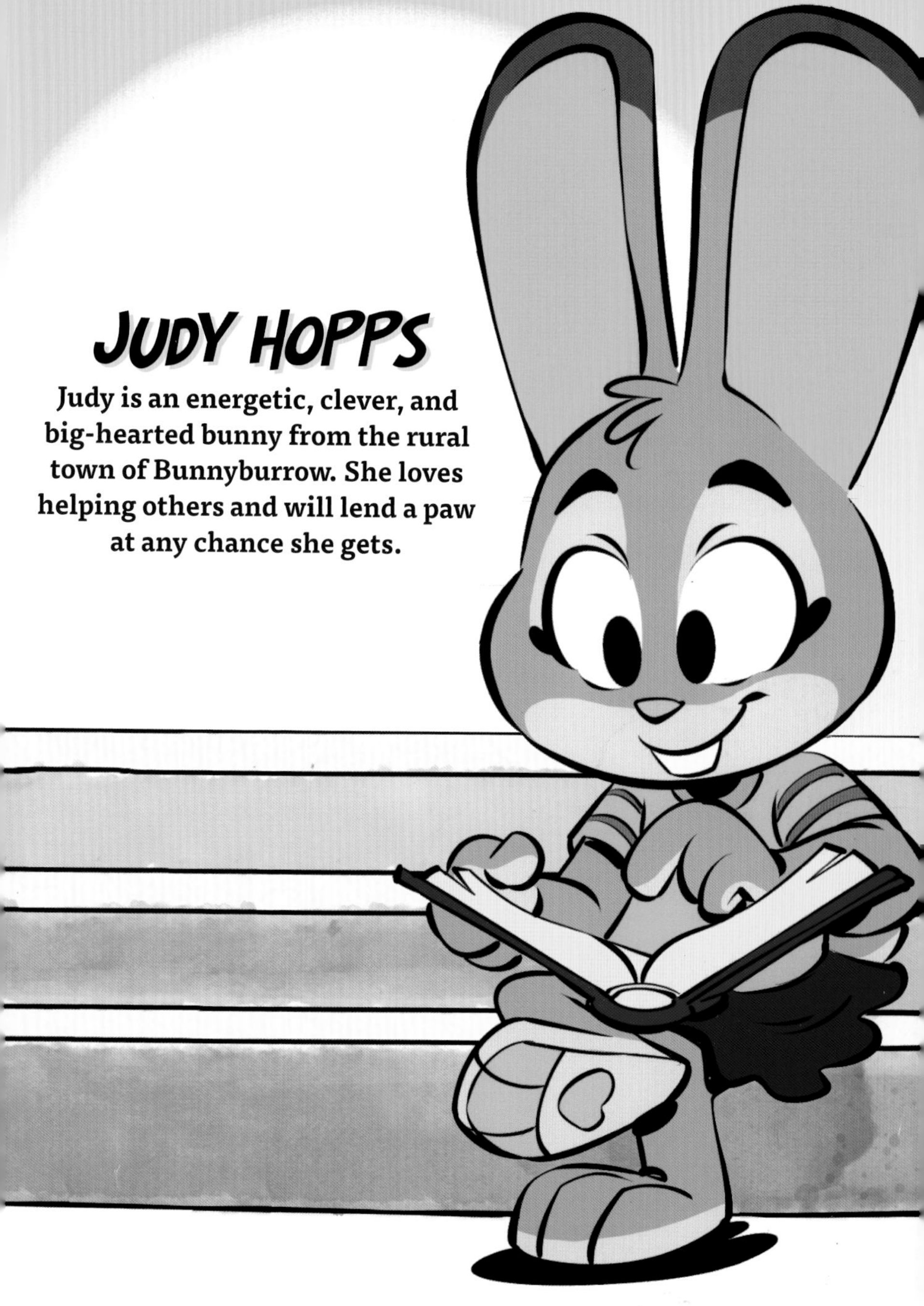

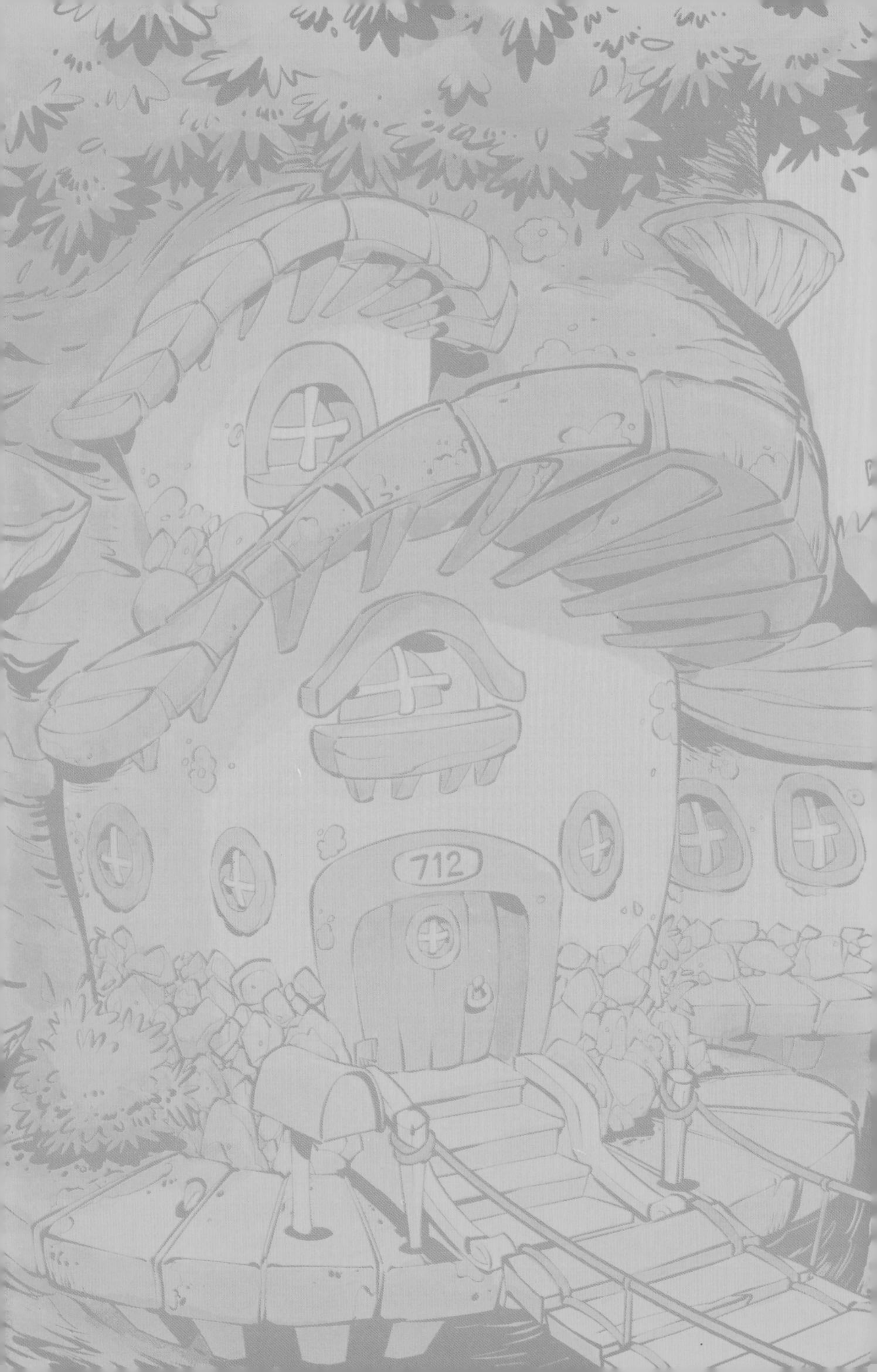
712

Judy in the Sky with Dinah

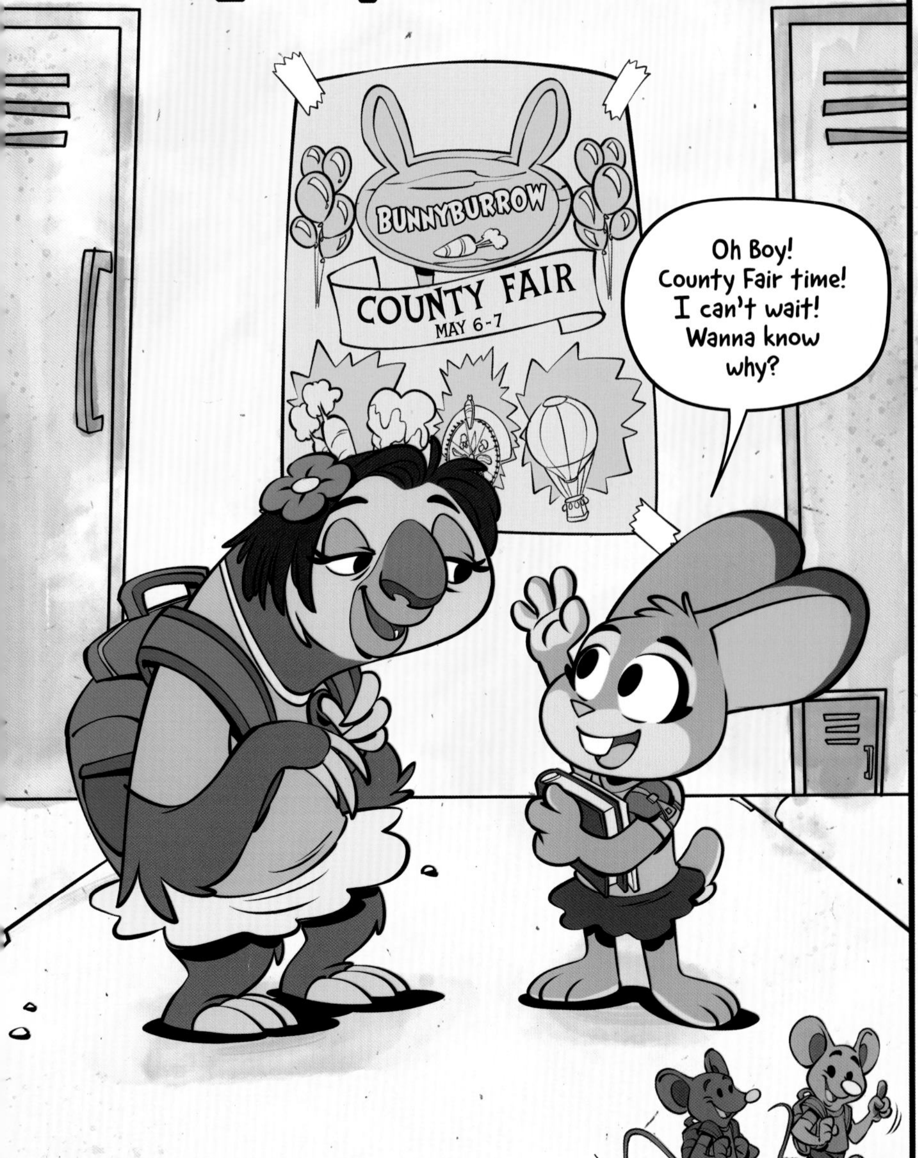
BUNNYBURROW
COUNTY FAIR
MAY 6-7
Oh Boy! County Fair time! I can't wait! Wanna know why?

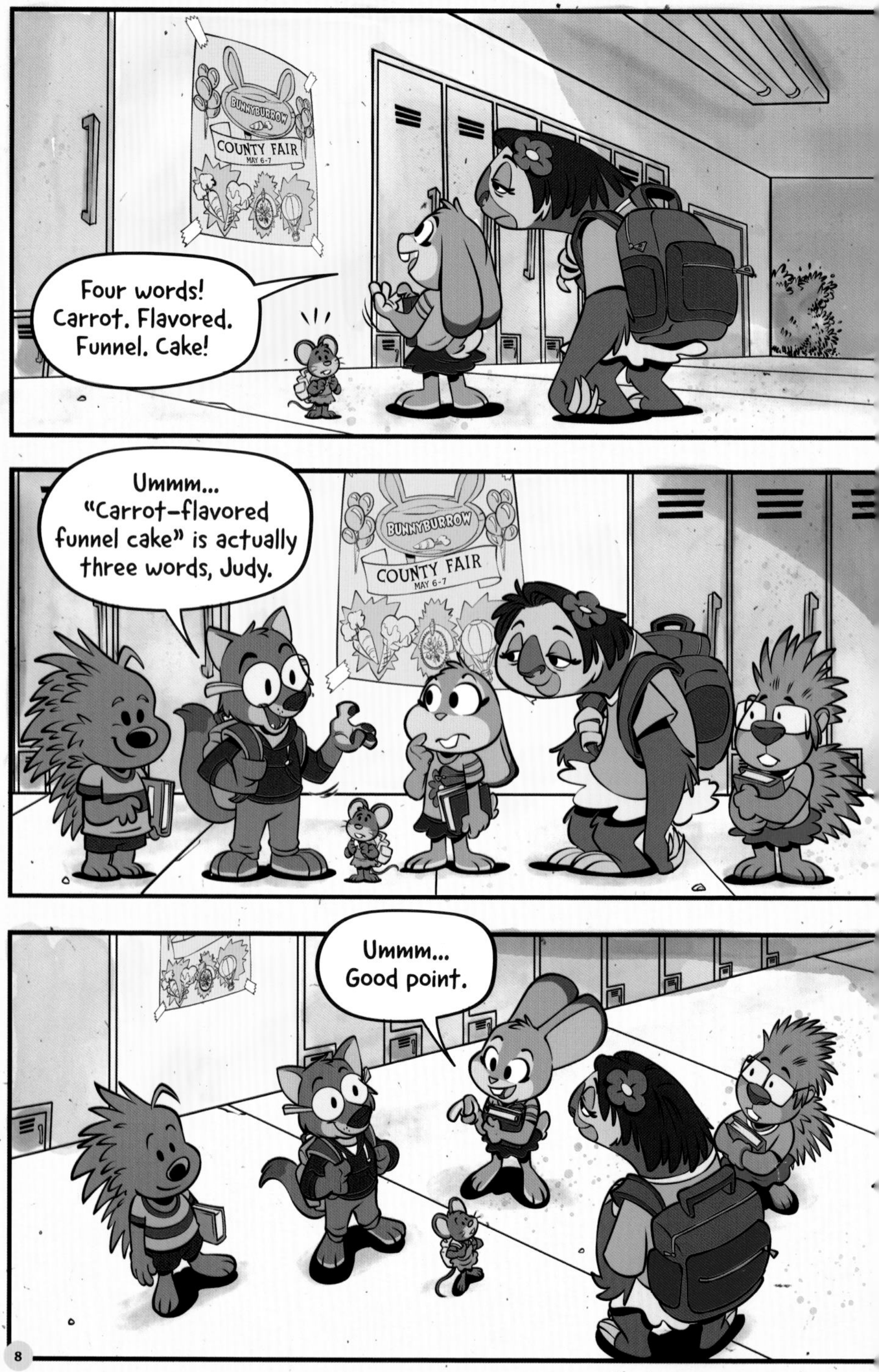
BUNNYBURROW
COUNTY FAIR
MAY 6-7
Four words! Carrot. Flavored. Funnel. Cake!
BUNNYBURROW
COUNTY FAIR
MAY 6-7
Ummm... "Carrot-flavored funnel cake" is actually three words, Judy.
Ummm... Good point.

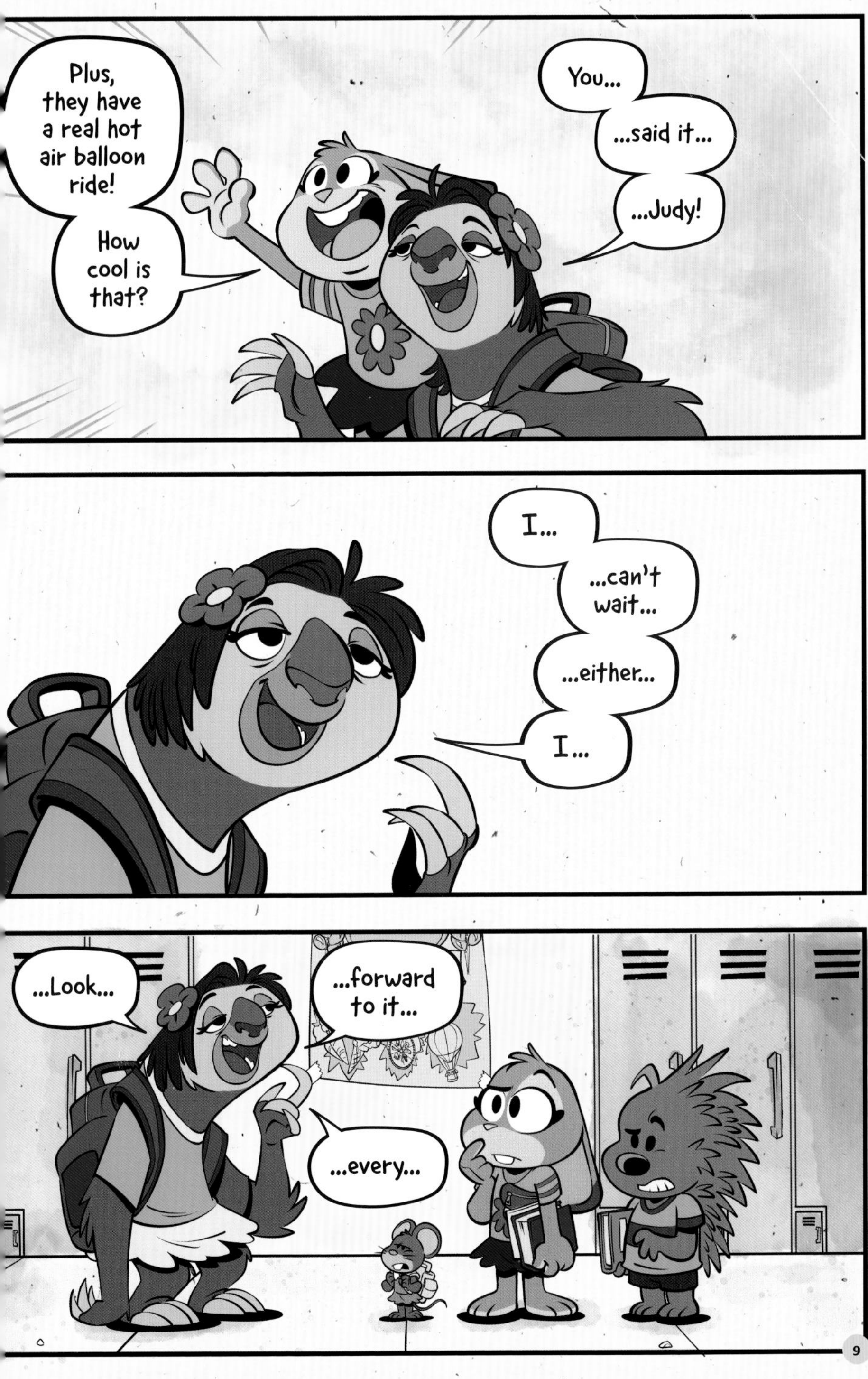

Plus, they have a real hot air balloon ride!
How cool is that?
You...
...said it...
...Judy!
I...
...can't wait...
...either...
I...
...Look...
...forward to it...
...every...

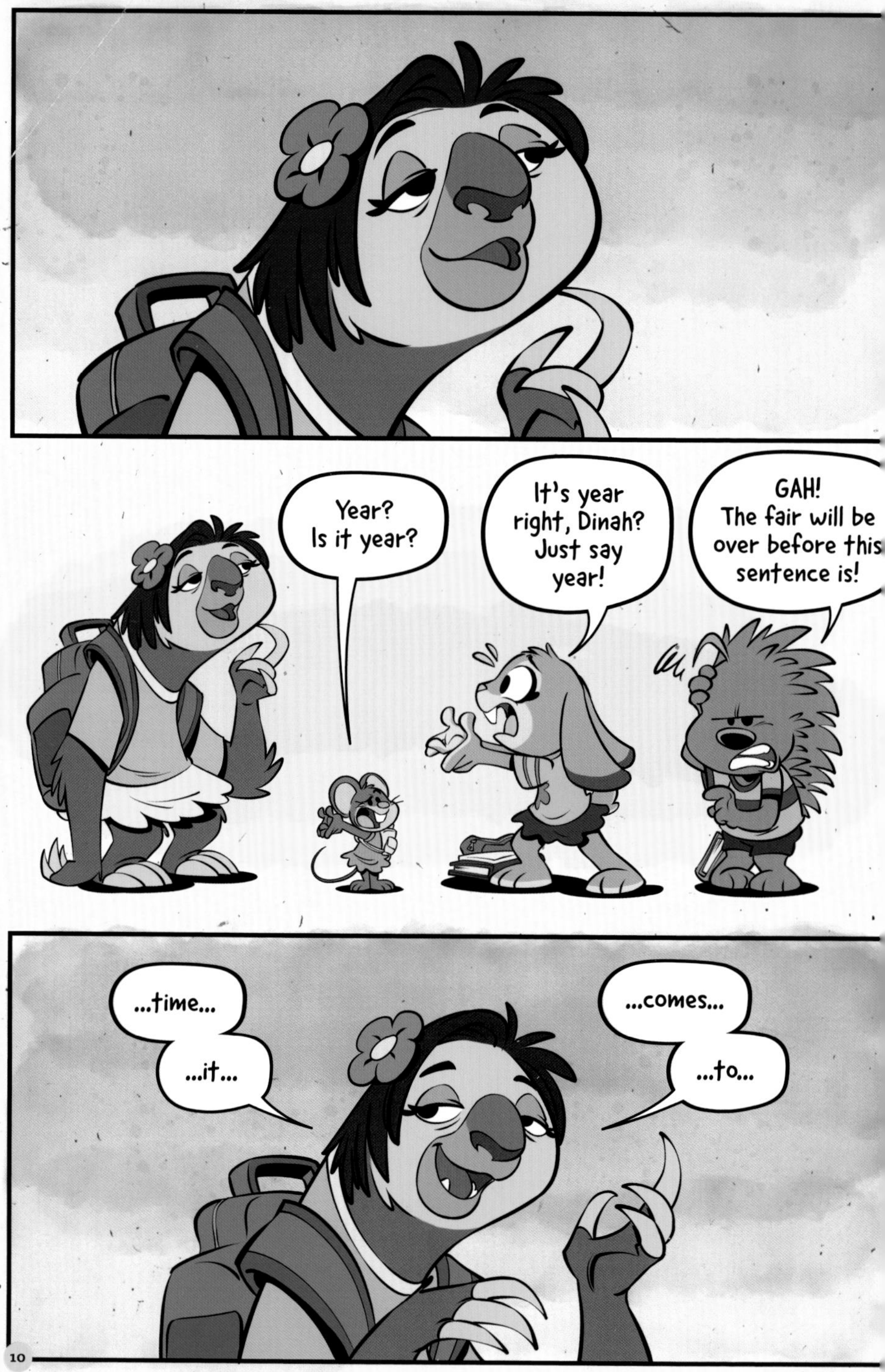
Year?
Is it year?
It's year
right, Dinah?
Just say
year!
GAH!
The fair will be
over before this
sentence is!
...time...
...it...
...comes...
...to...

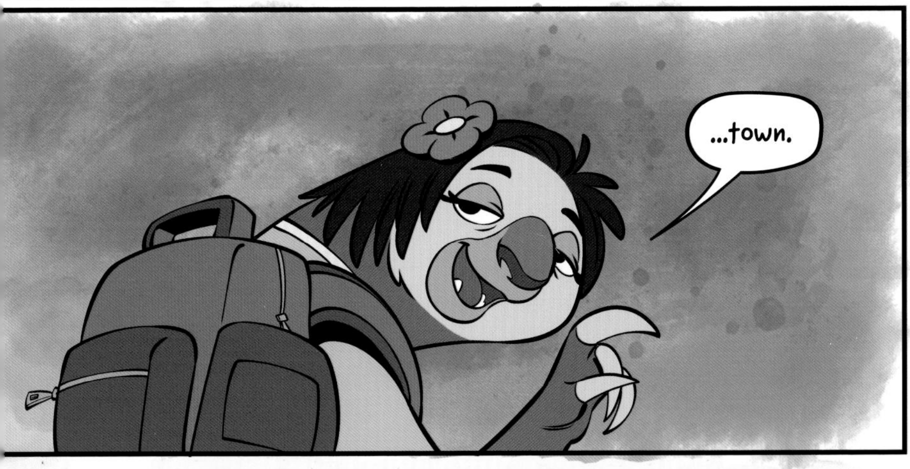
...town.

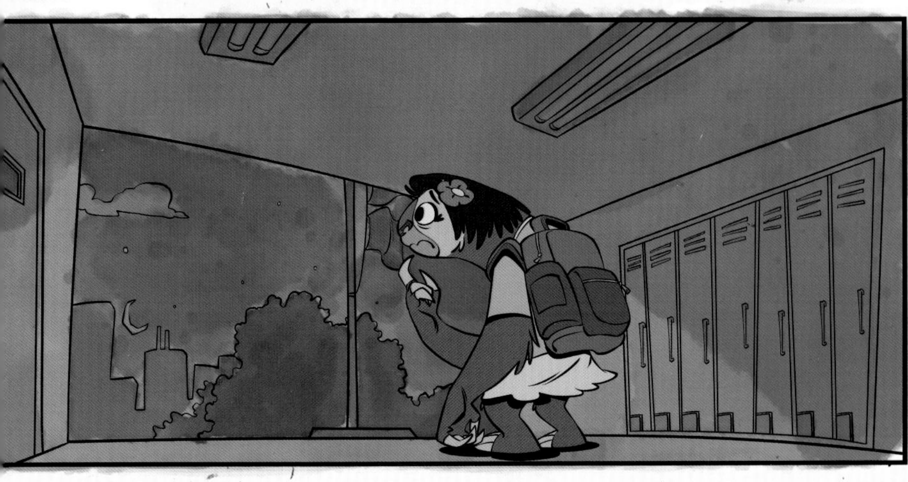

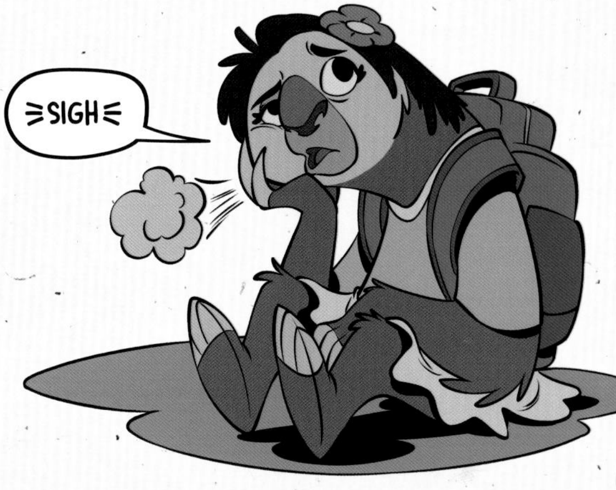
SIGH

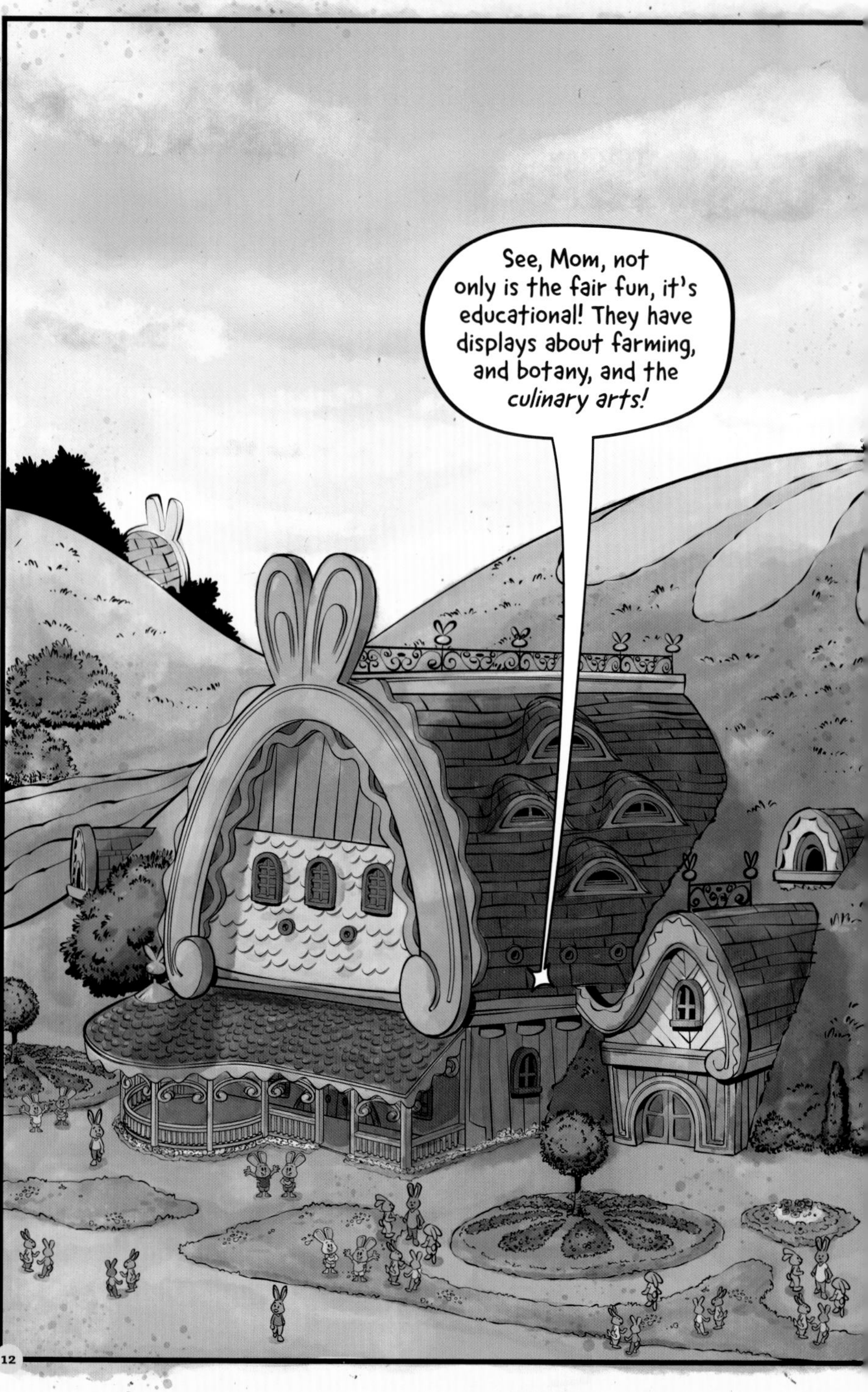
See, Mom, not only is the fair fun, it's educational! They have displays about farming, and botany, and the *culinary arts!*

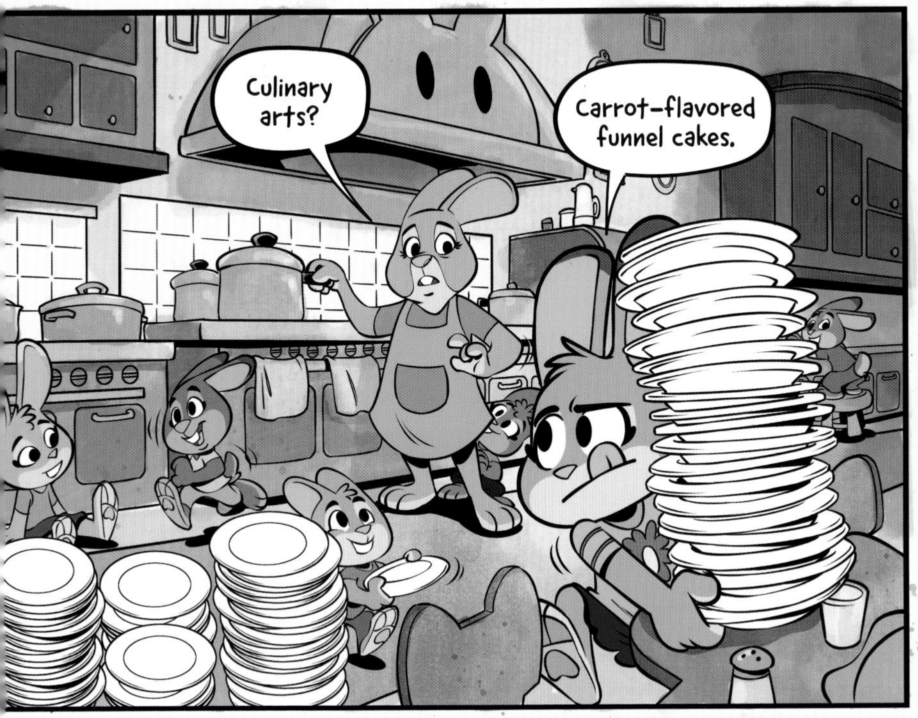
Culinary arts?
Carrot-flavored funnel cakes.

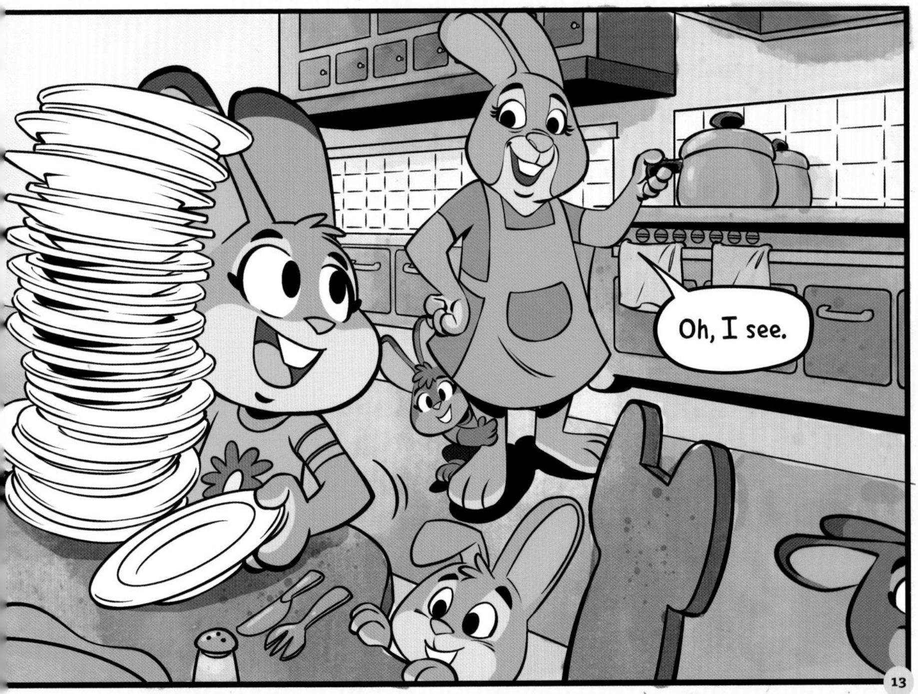
Oh, I see.

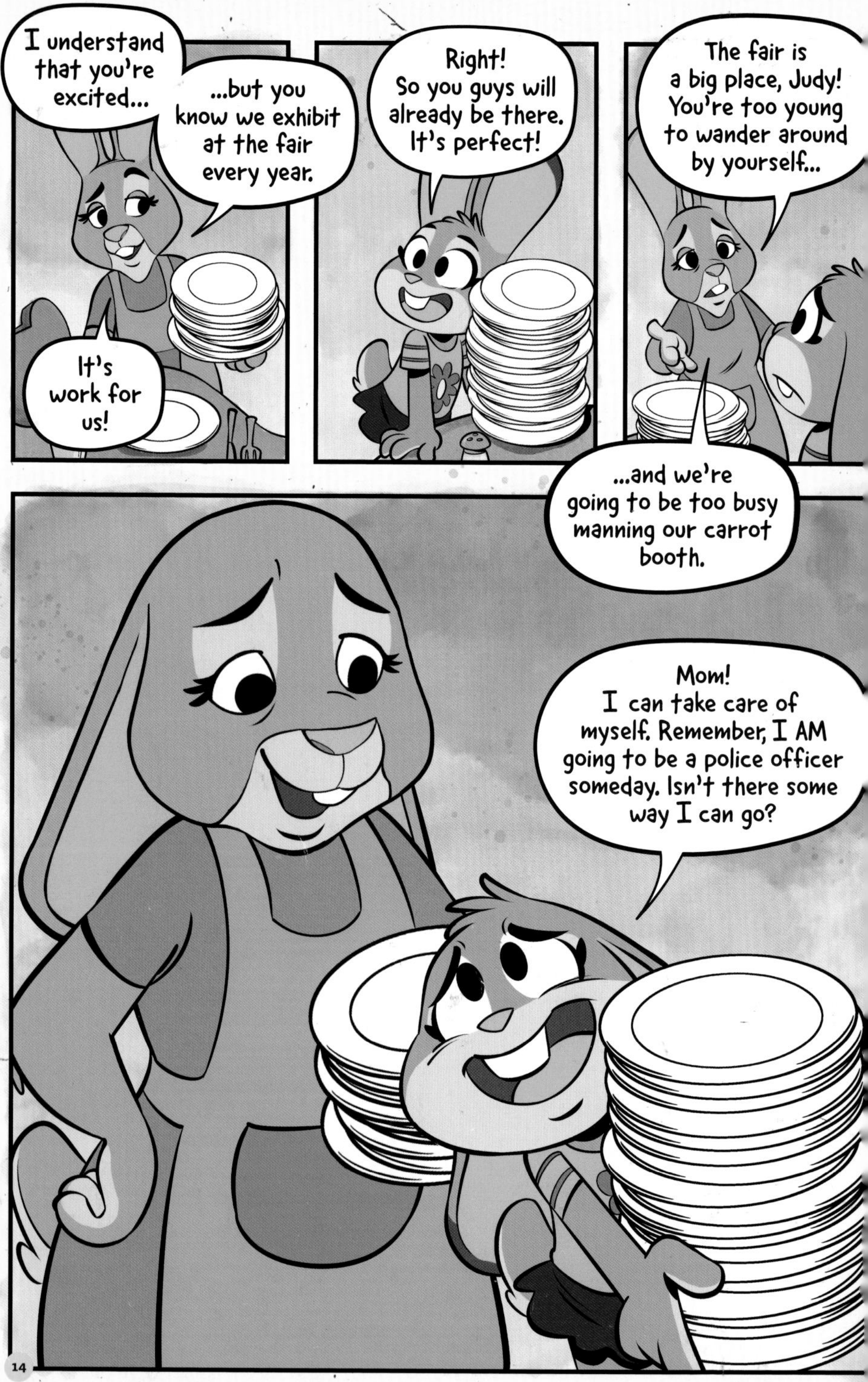
I understand that you're excited...
...but you know we exhibit at the fair every year.
It's work for us!
Right! So you guys will already be there. It's perfect!
The fair is a big place, Judy! You're too young to wander around by yourself...
...and we're going to be too busy manning our carrot booth.
Mom! I can take care of myself. Remember, I AM going to be a police officer someday. Isn't there some way I can go?

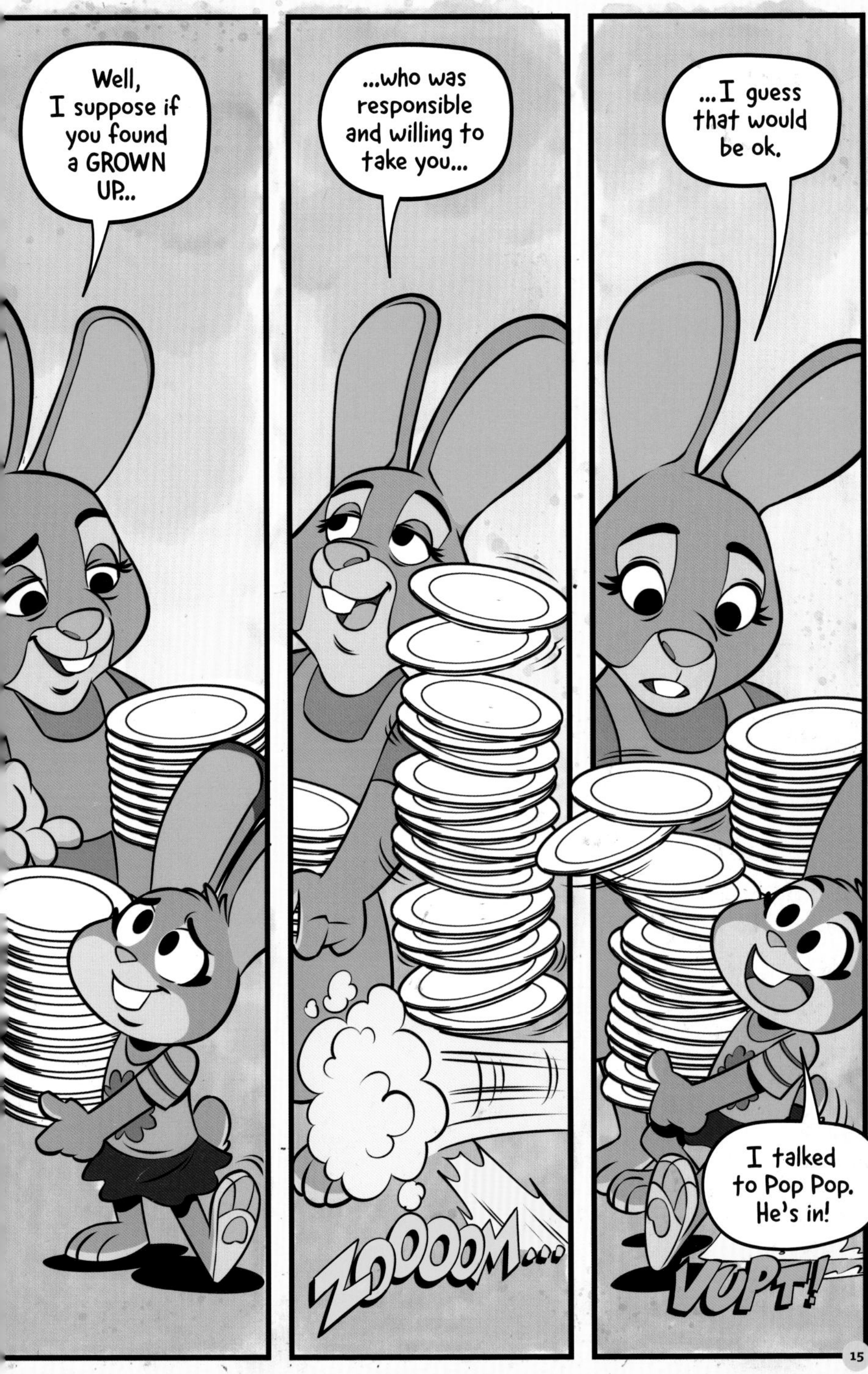
Well, I suppose if you found a GROWN UP...
...who was responsible and willing to take you...
ZOOOOM...
...I guess that would be ok.
I talked to Pop Pop. He's in!
VUPT!

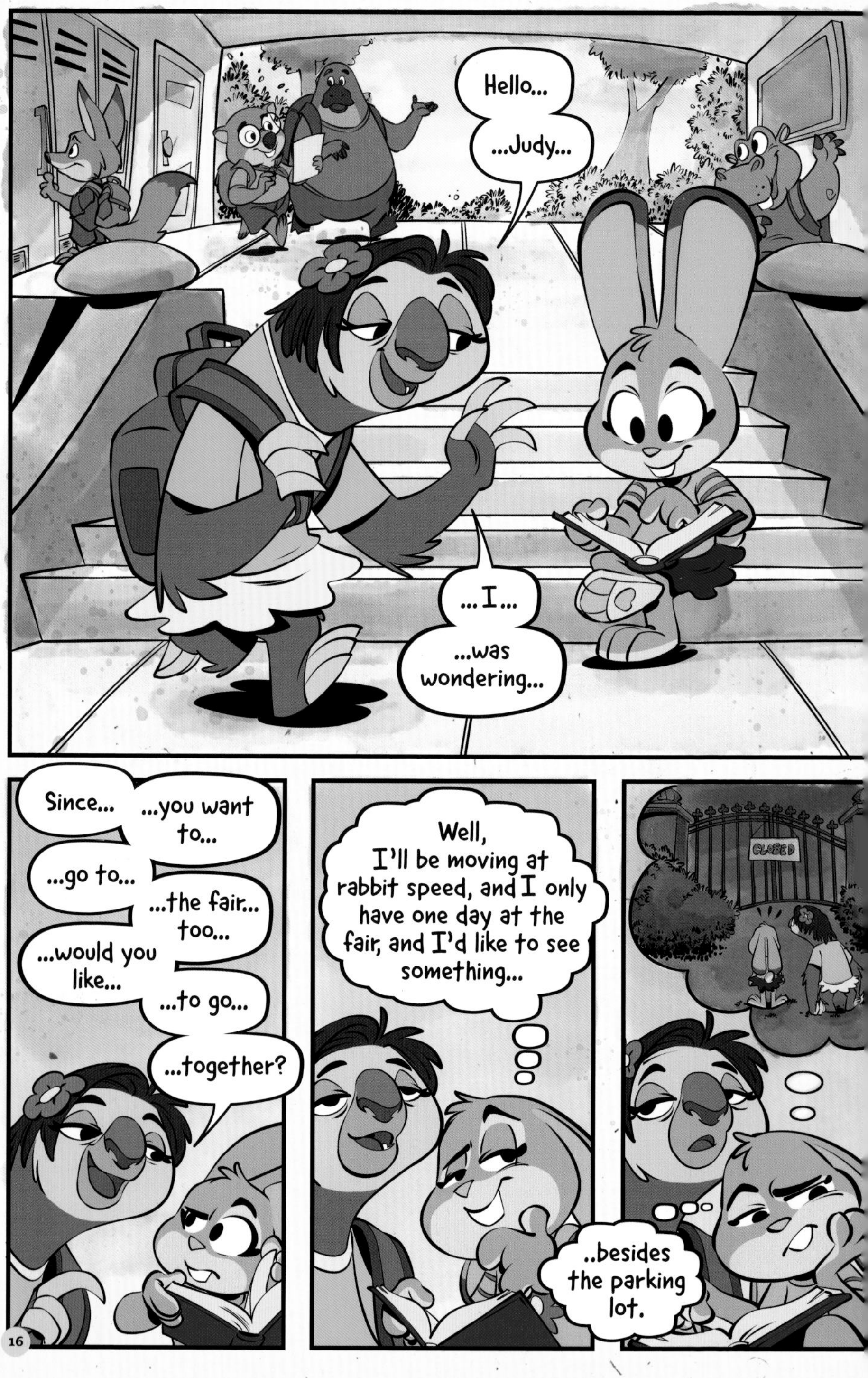
Hello...
...Judy...
...I...
...was wondering...
Since...
...you want to...
...go to...
...the fair... too...
...would you like...
...to go...
...together?
Well, I'll be moving at rabbit speed, and I only have one day at the fair, and I'd like to see something...
CLOSED
..besides the parking lot.

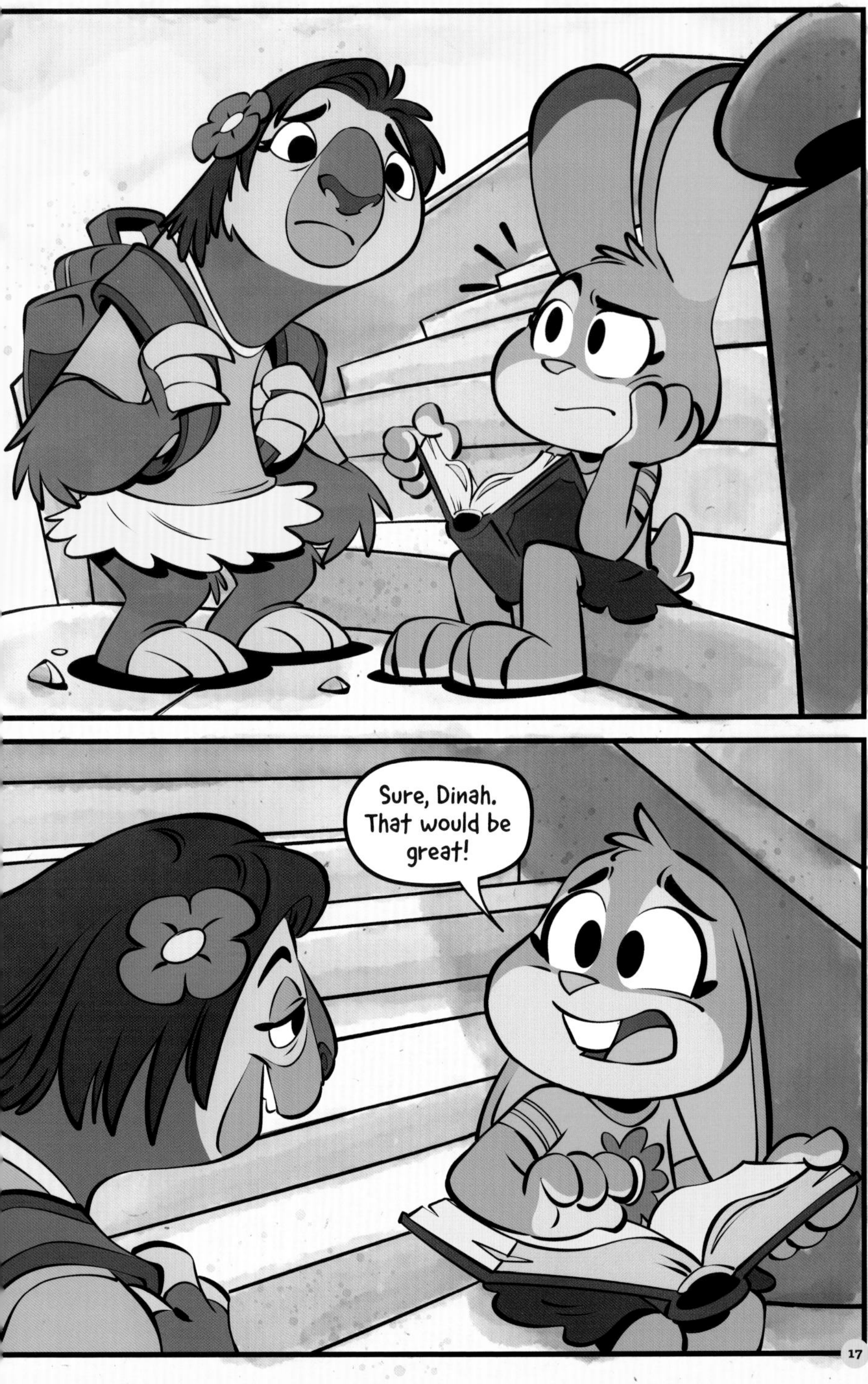
Sure, Dinah. That would be great!

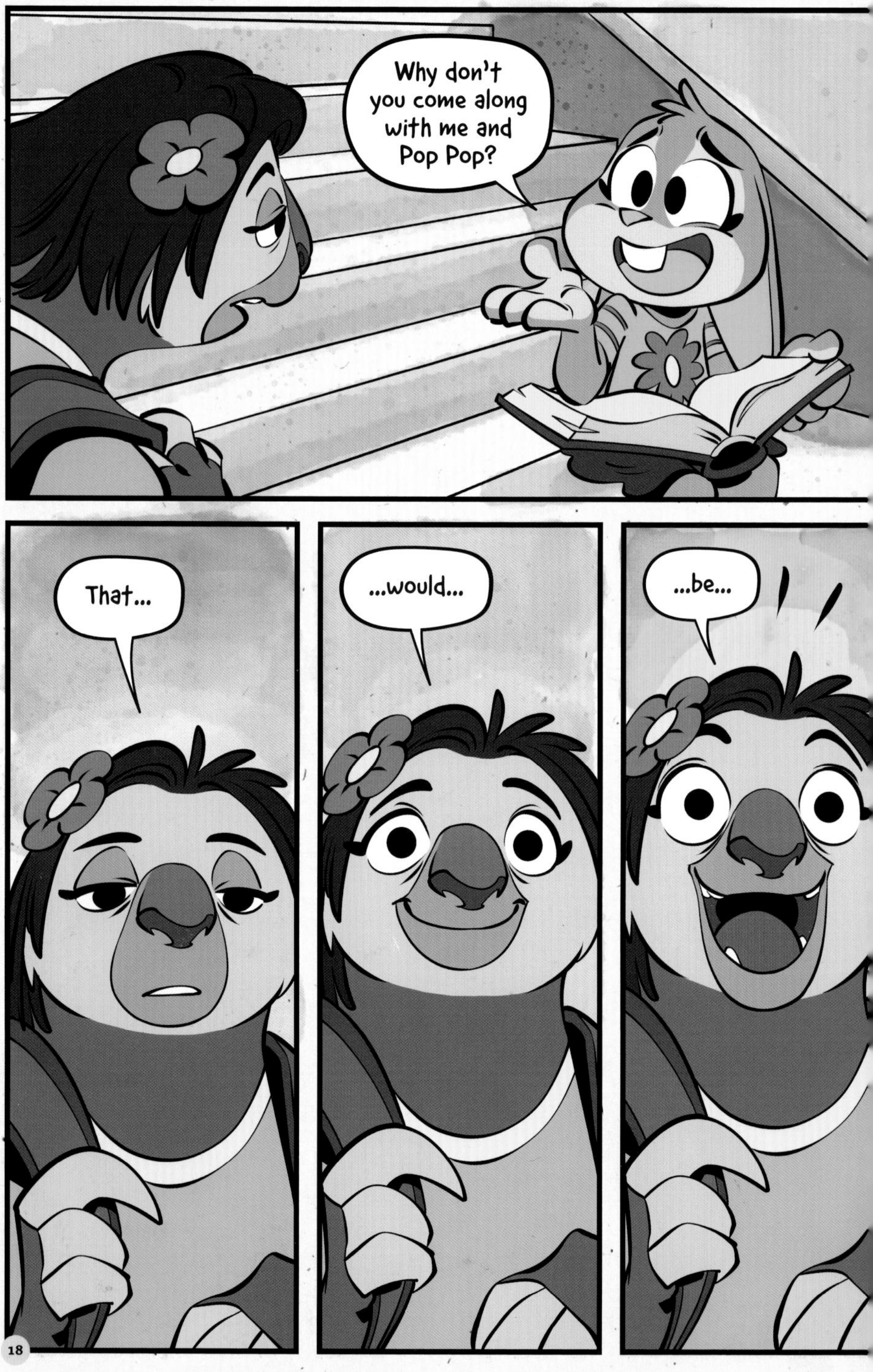
Why don't you come along with me and Pop Pop?
That...
...would...
...be...

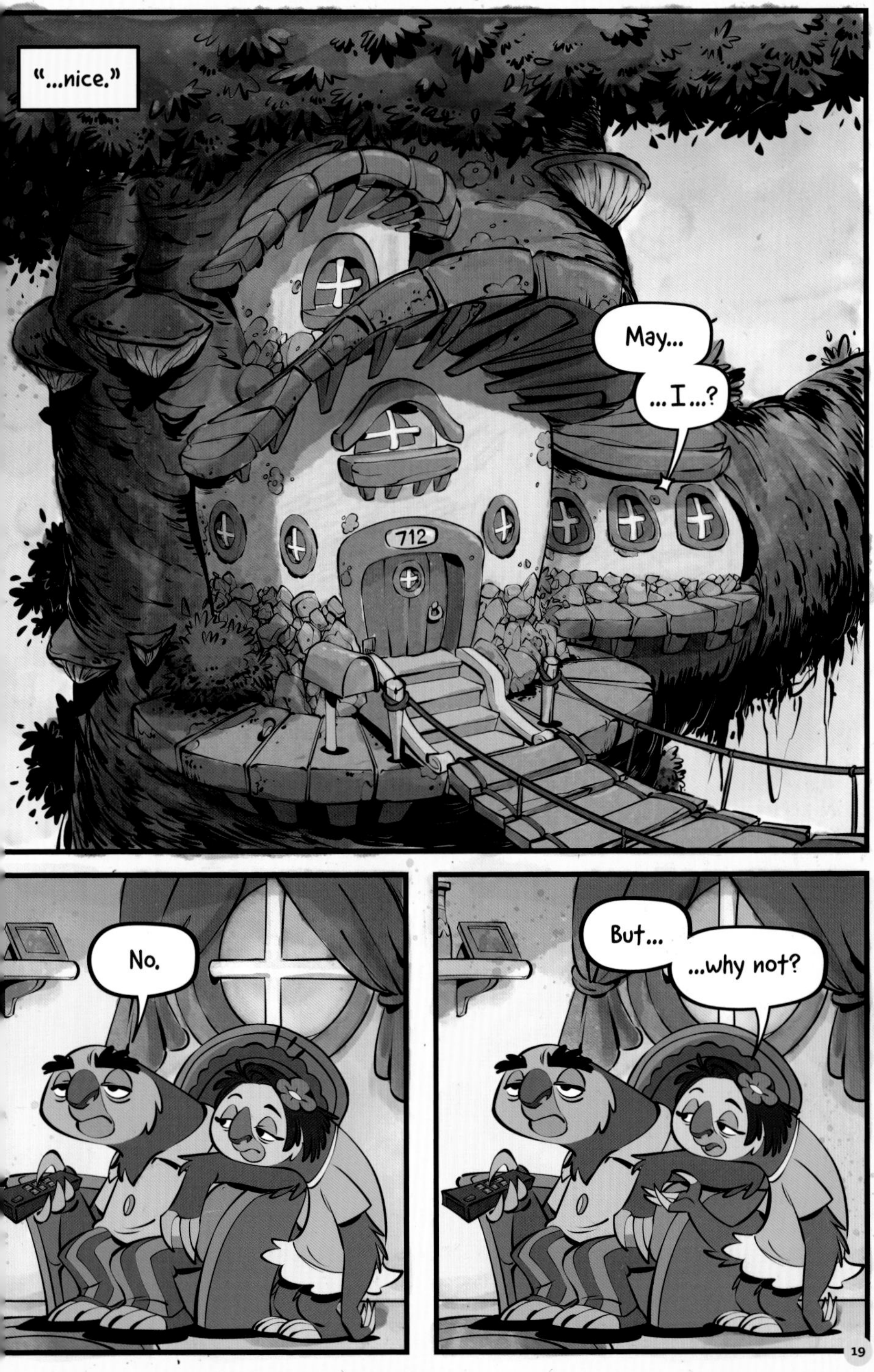
"...nice."
712
May...
...I...?
No.
But...
...why not?

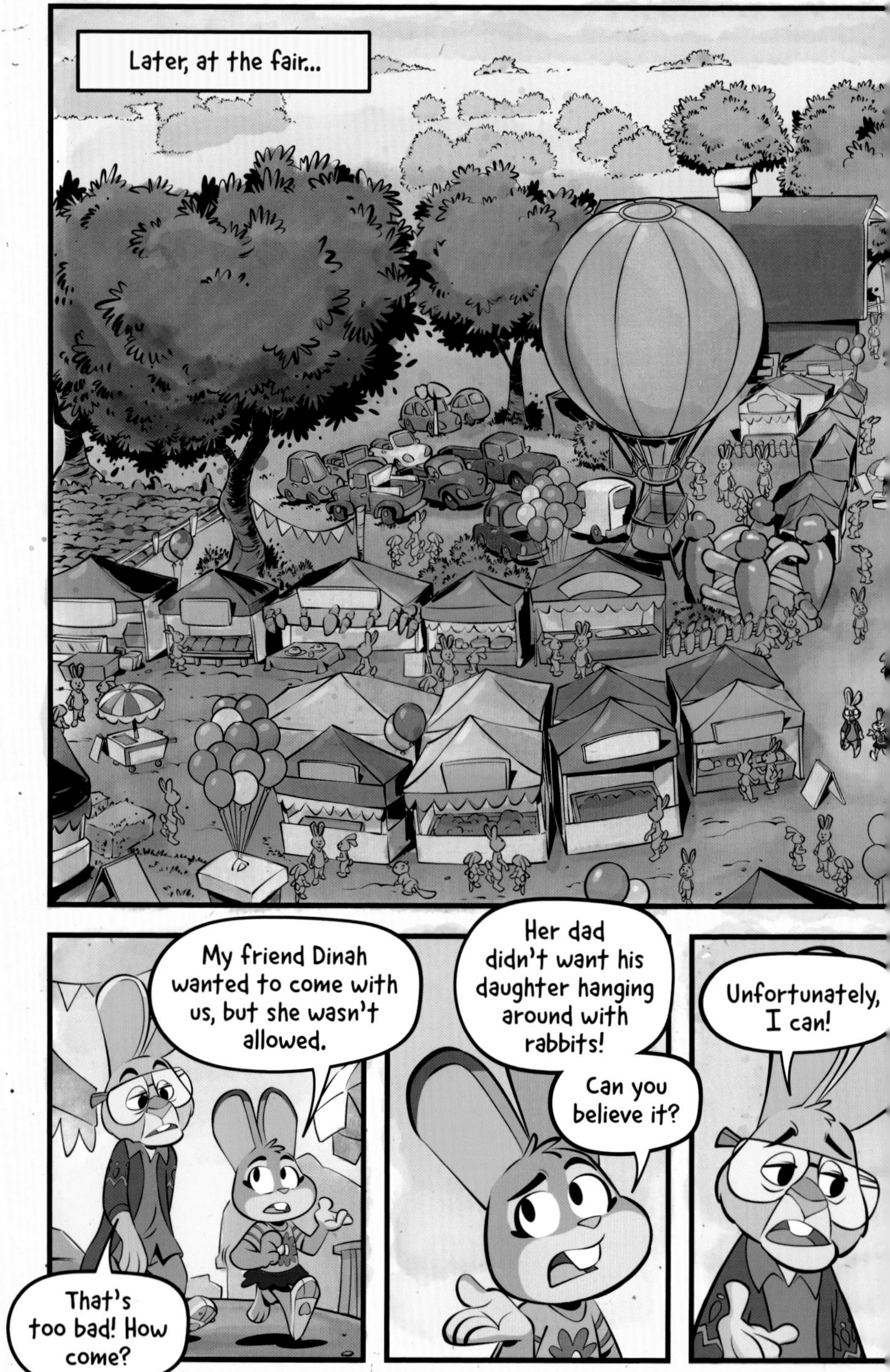

Later, at the fair...
My friend Dinah wanted to come with us, but she wasn't allowed.
That's too bad! How come?
Her dad didn't want his daughter hanging around with rabbits!
Can you believe it?
Unfortunately, I can!

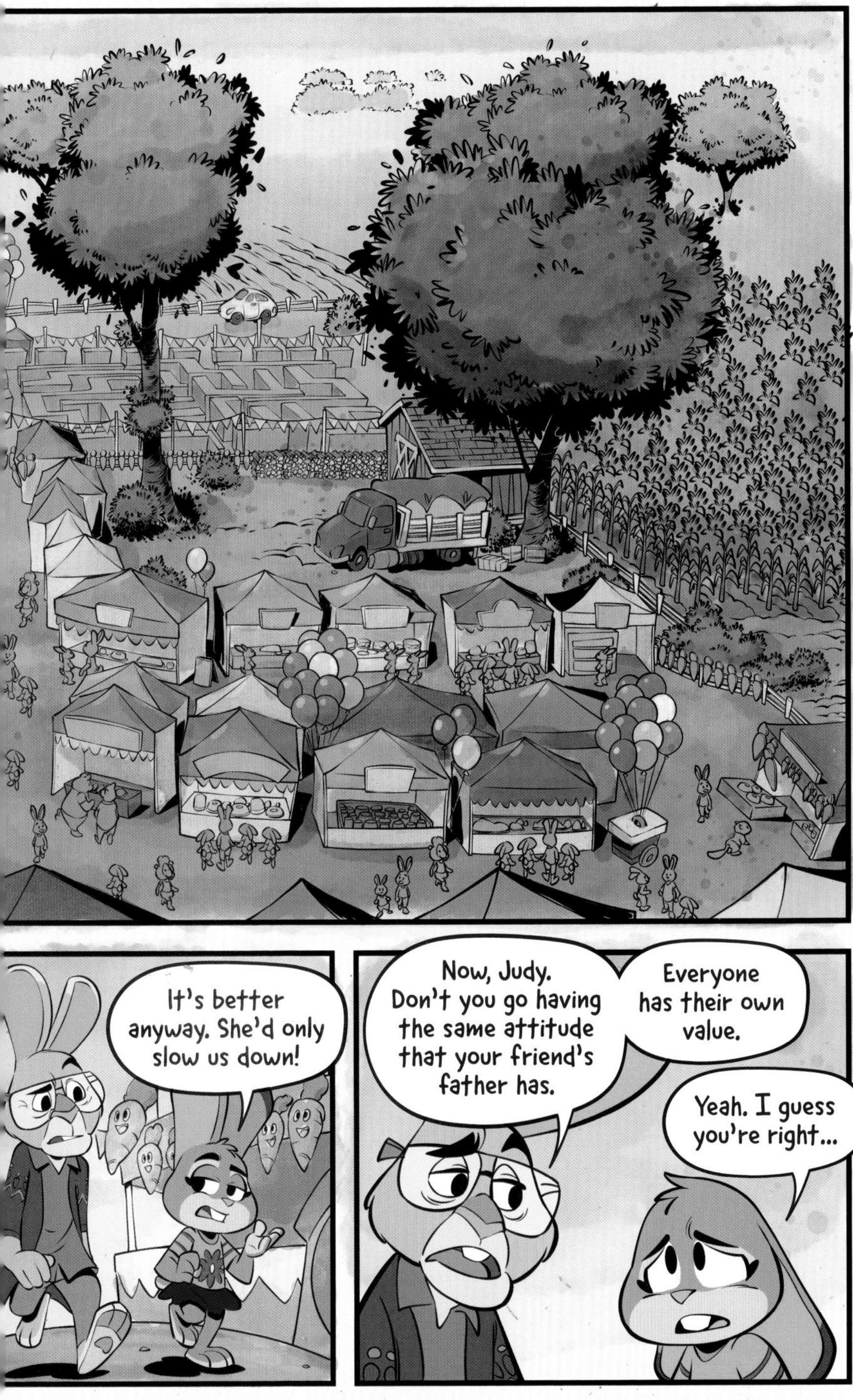
It's better anyway. She'd only slow us down!
Now, Judy. Don't you go having the same attitude that your friend's father has.
Everyone has their own value.
Yeah. I guess you're right...

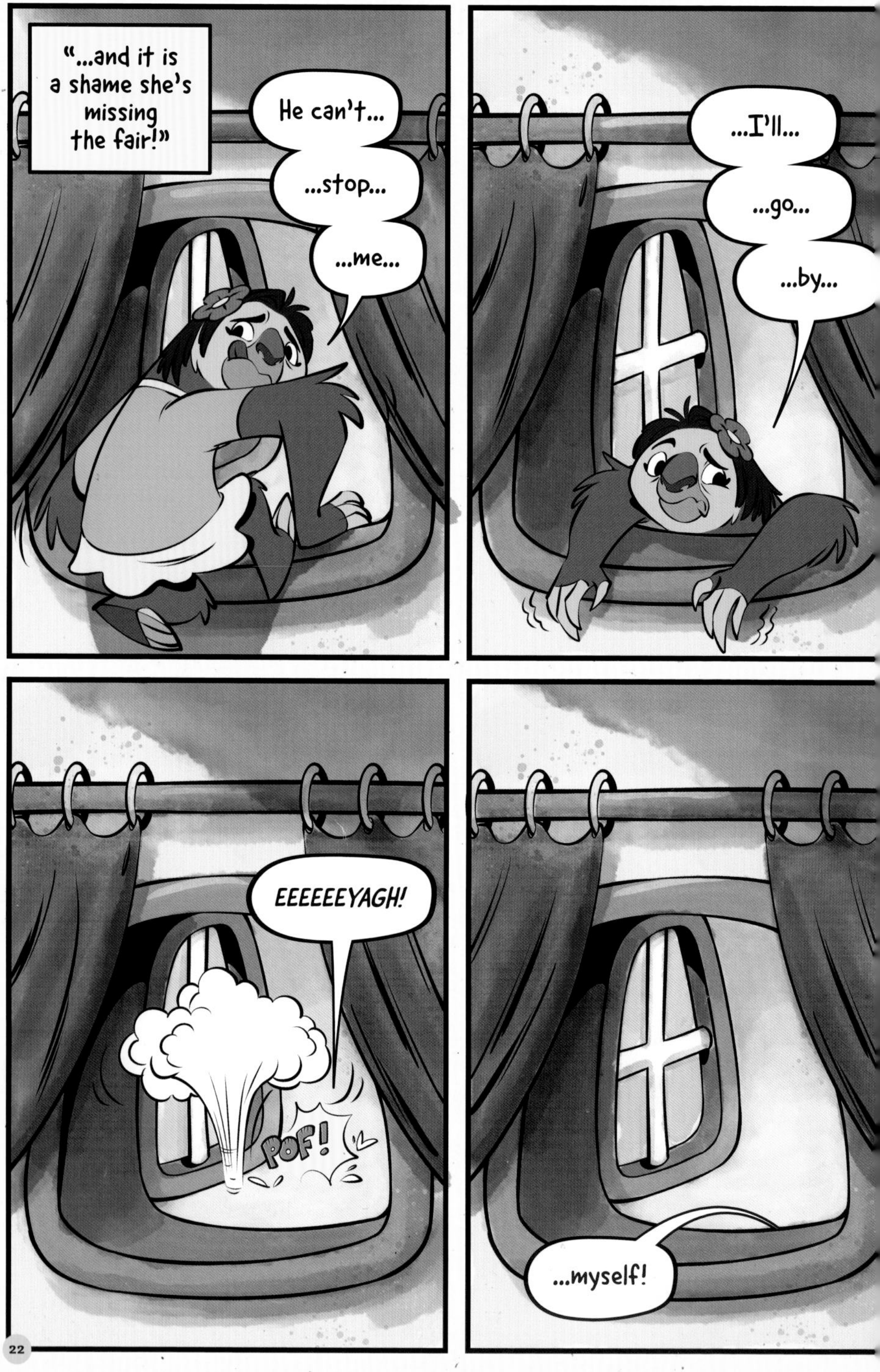
"...and it is a shame she's missing the fair!"
He can't...
...stop...
...me...
...I'll...
...go...
...by...
EEEEEEYAGH!
POF!
...myself!

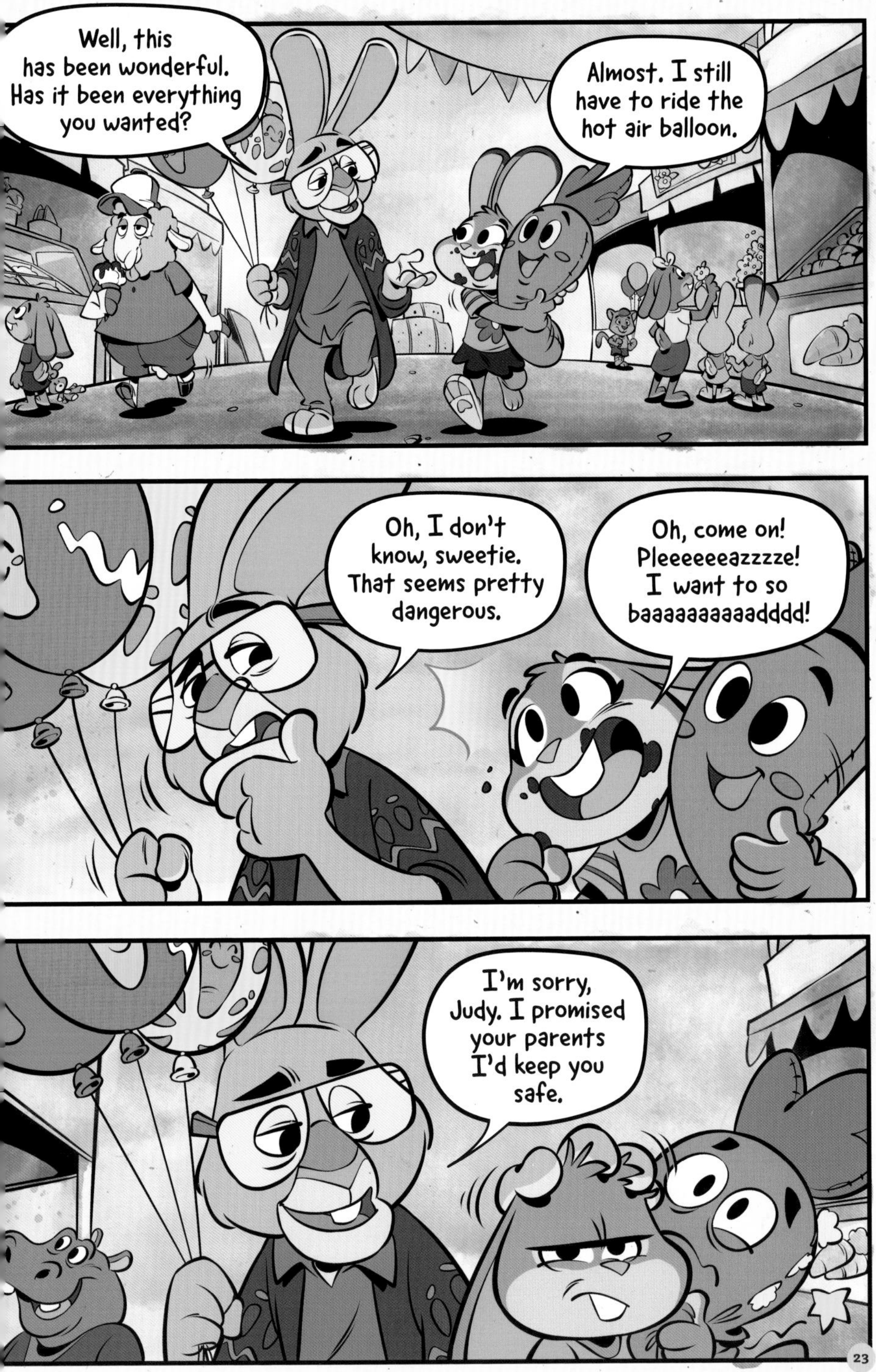
Well, this has been wonderful. Has it been everything you wanted?
Almost. I still have to ride the hot air balloon.
Oh, I don't know, sweetie. That seems pretty dangerous.
Oh, come on! Pleeeeeeazzzze! I want to so baaaaaaaaaadddd!
I'm sorry, Judy. I promised your parents I'd keep you safe.

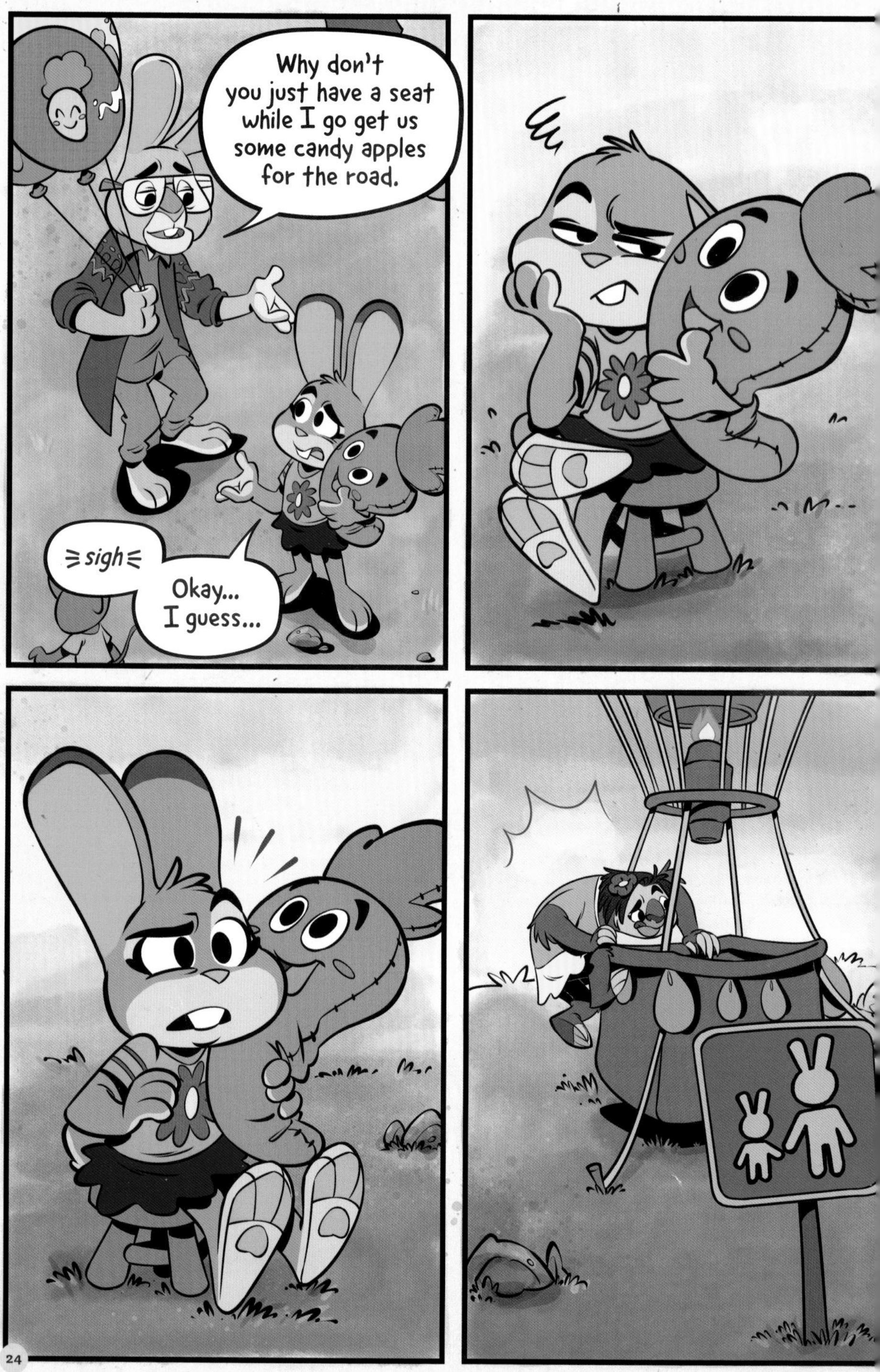
Why don't you just have a seat while I go get us some candy apples for the road.
≋sigh≋
Okay... I guess...

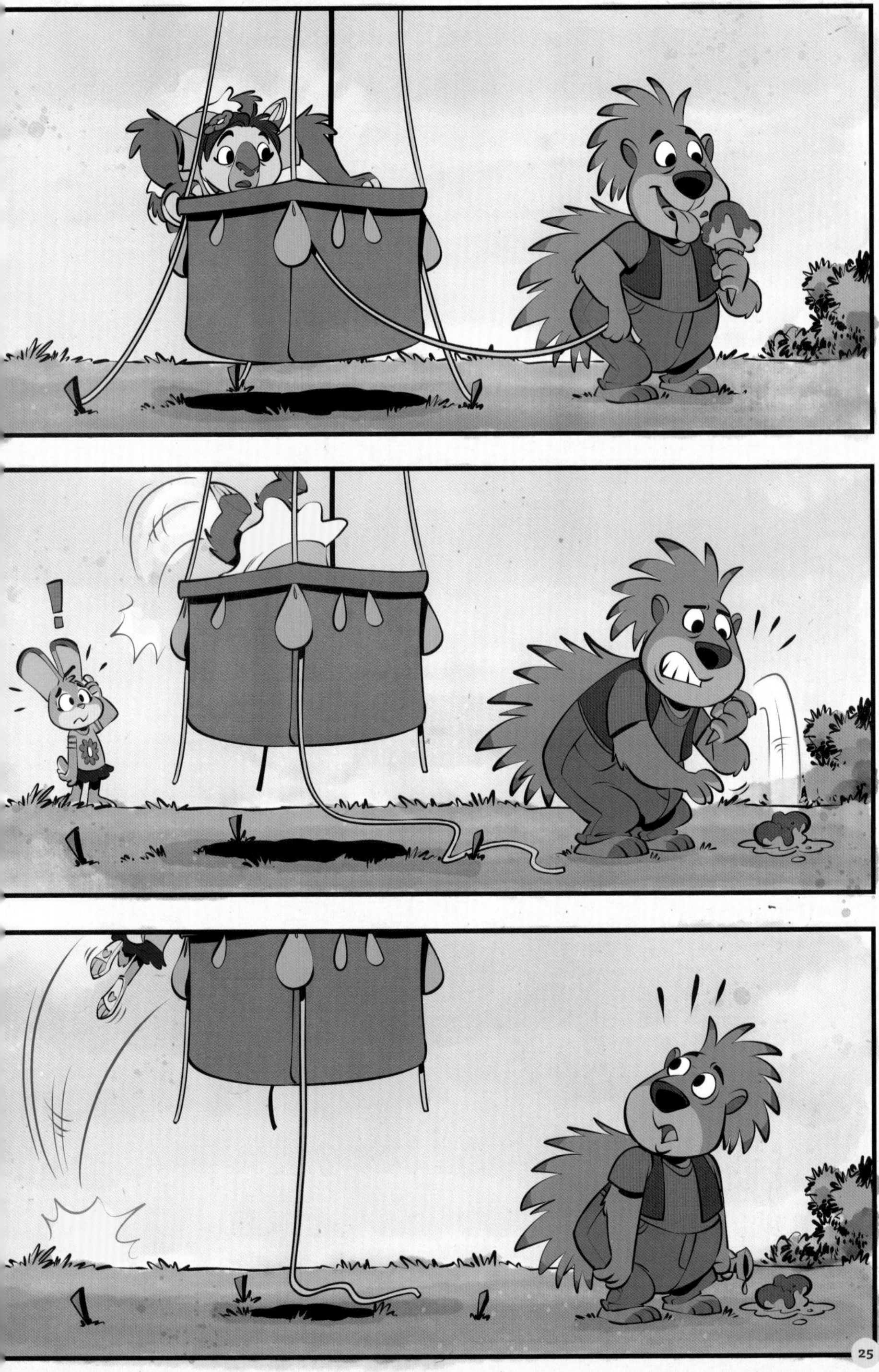
!

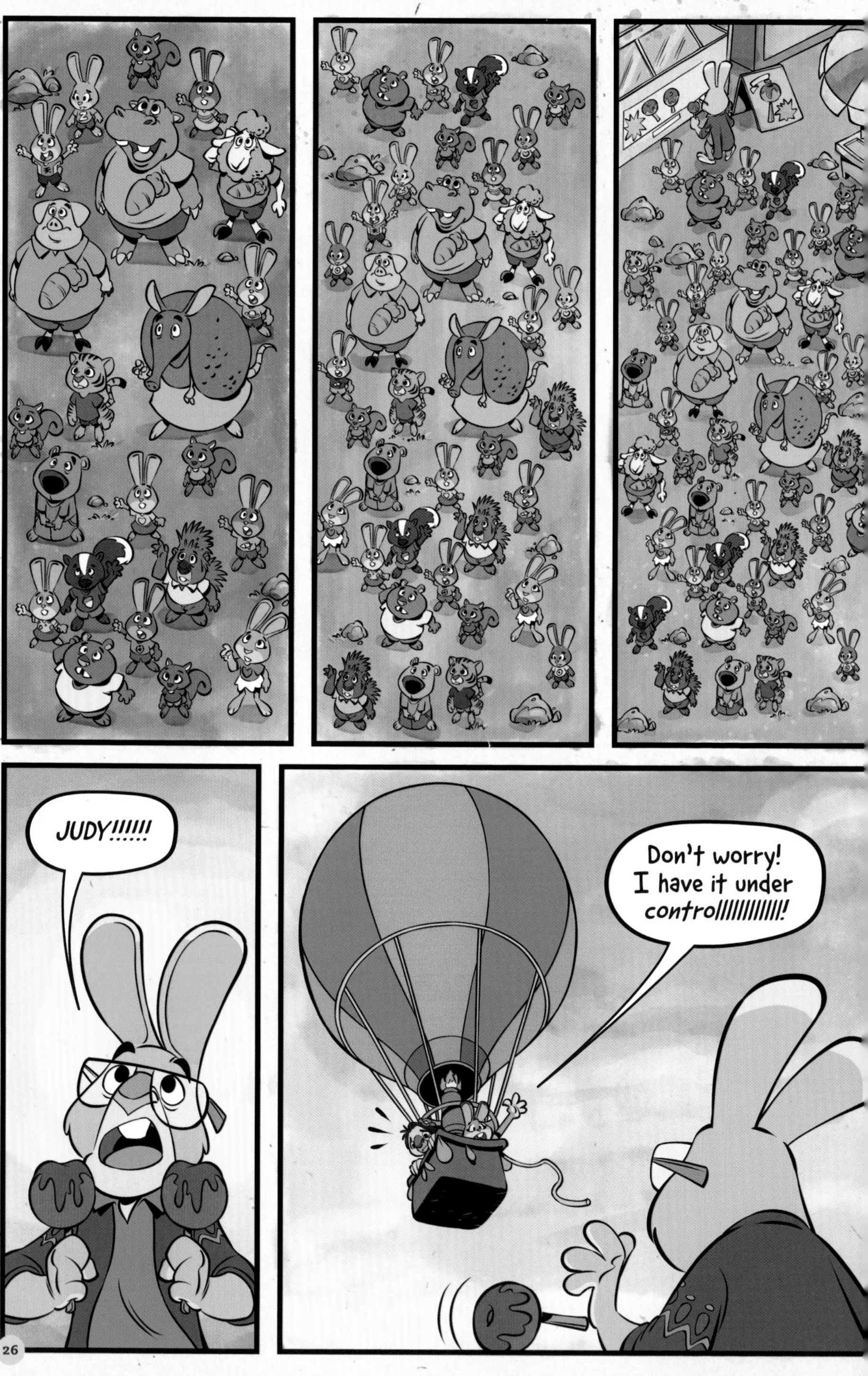

JUDY!!!!!!
Don't worry! I have it under control!!!!!!!!!!!!

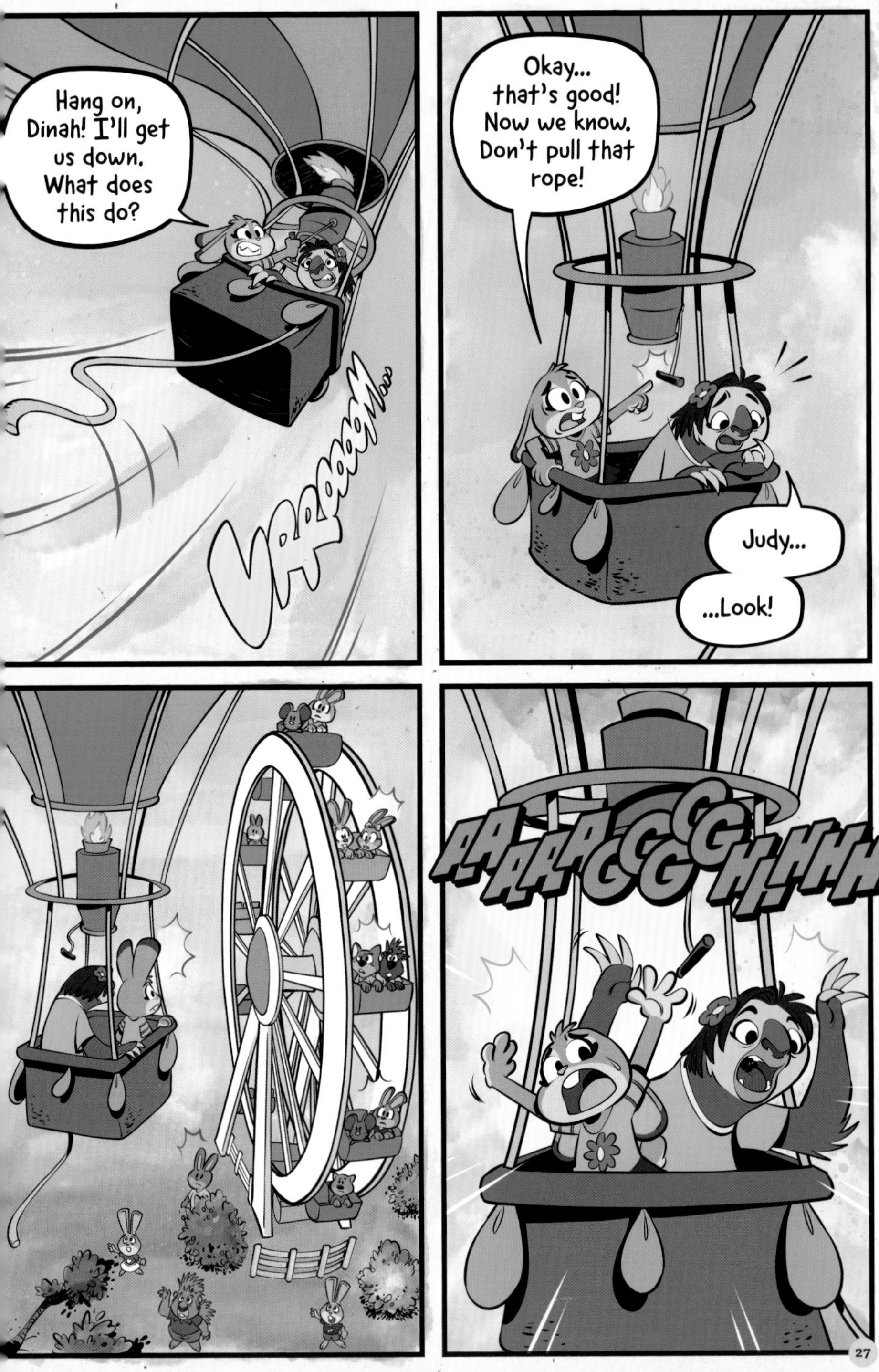
Hang on, Dinah! I'll get us down. What does this do?
VRROOOOOM
Okay... that's good! Now we know. Don't pull that rope!
Judy...
...Look!
AAAAAGGGGHHHHH

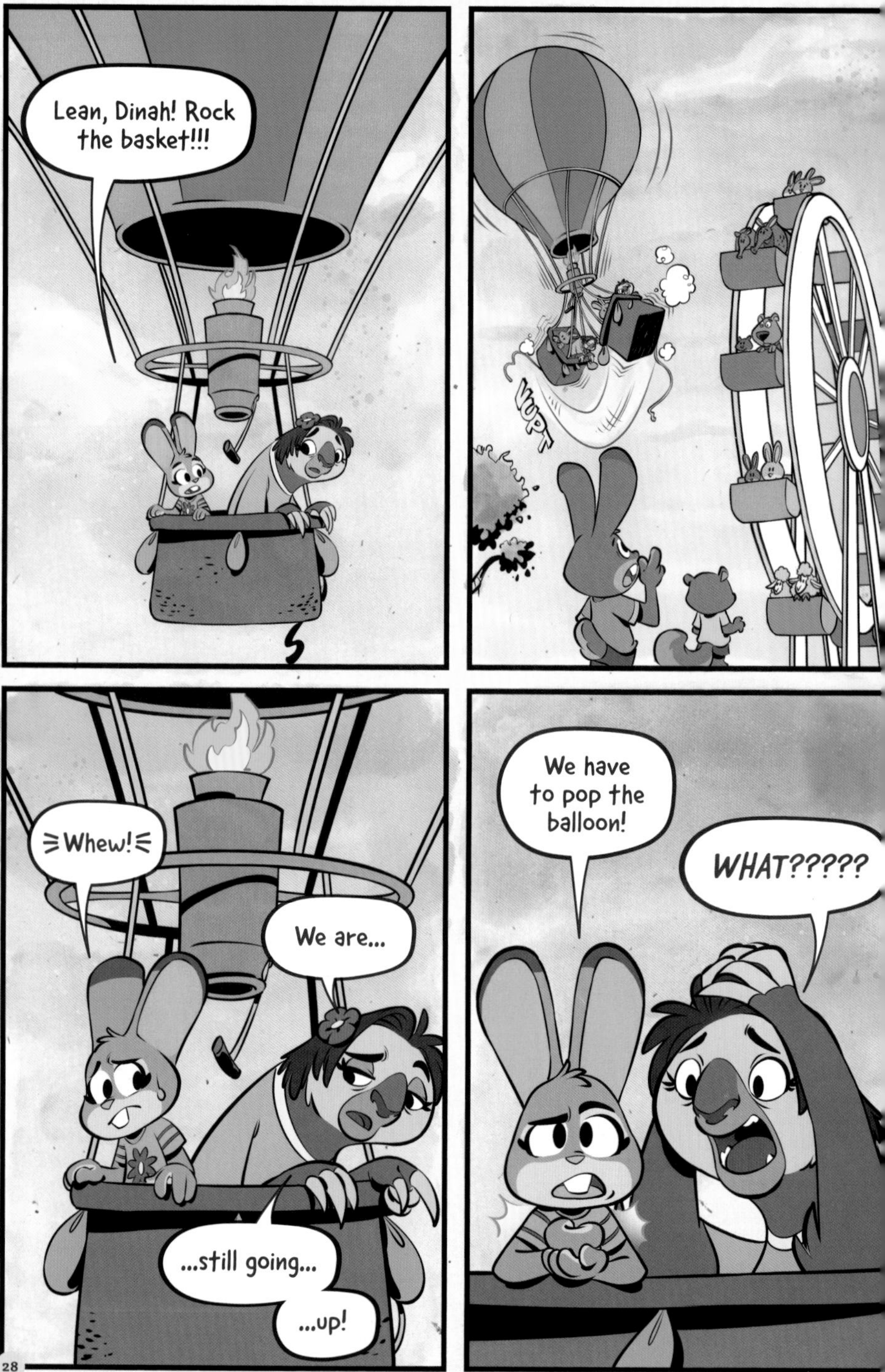
Lean, Dinah! Rock the basket!!!
VUPT
Whew!
We are...
...still going...
...up!
We have to pop the balloon!
WHAT?????

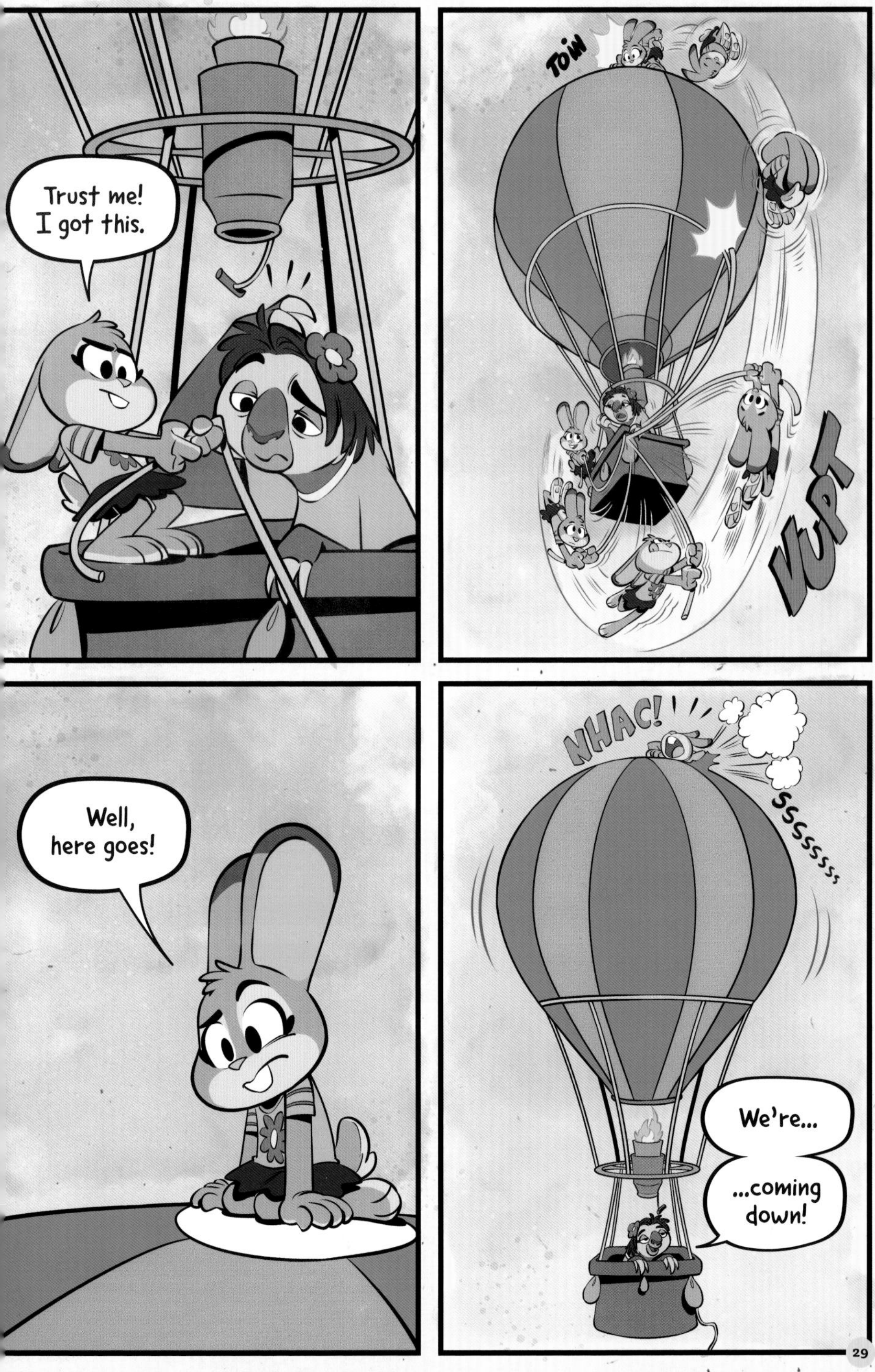
Trust me! I got this.
TOIN
VUPT
Well, here goes!
NHAC!
SSSSSSSS
We're...
...coming down!

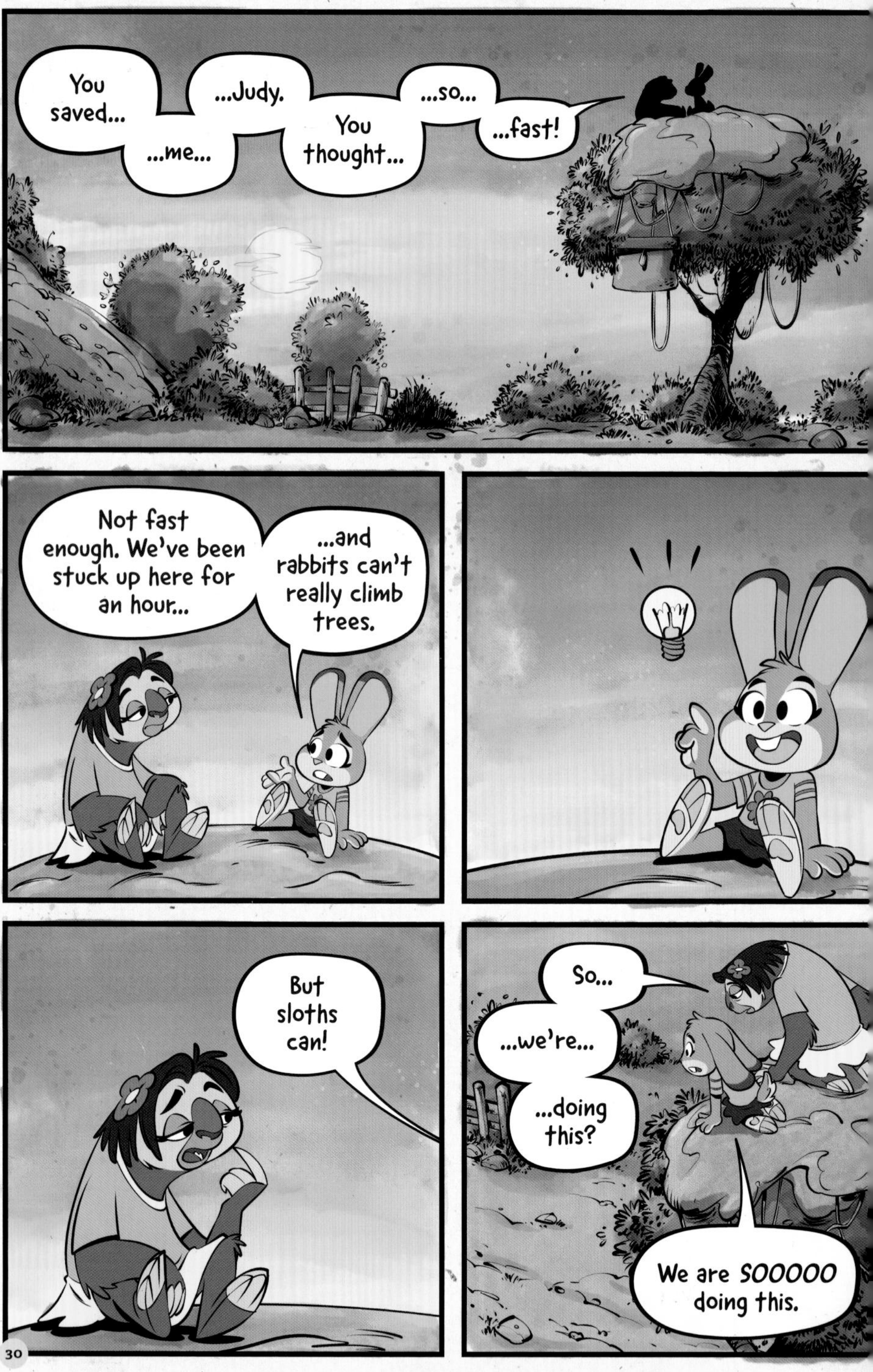
You saved...
...me...
...Judy.
You thought...
...so...
...fast!
Not fast enough. We've been stuck up here for an hour...
...and rabbits can't really climb trees.
But sloths can!
So...
...we're...
...doing this?
We are SOOOOO doing this.

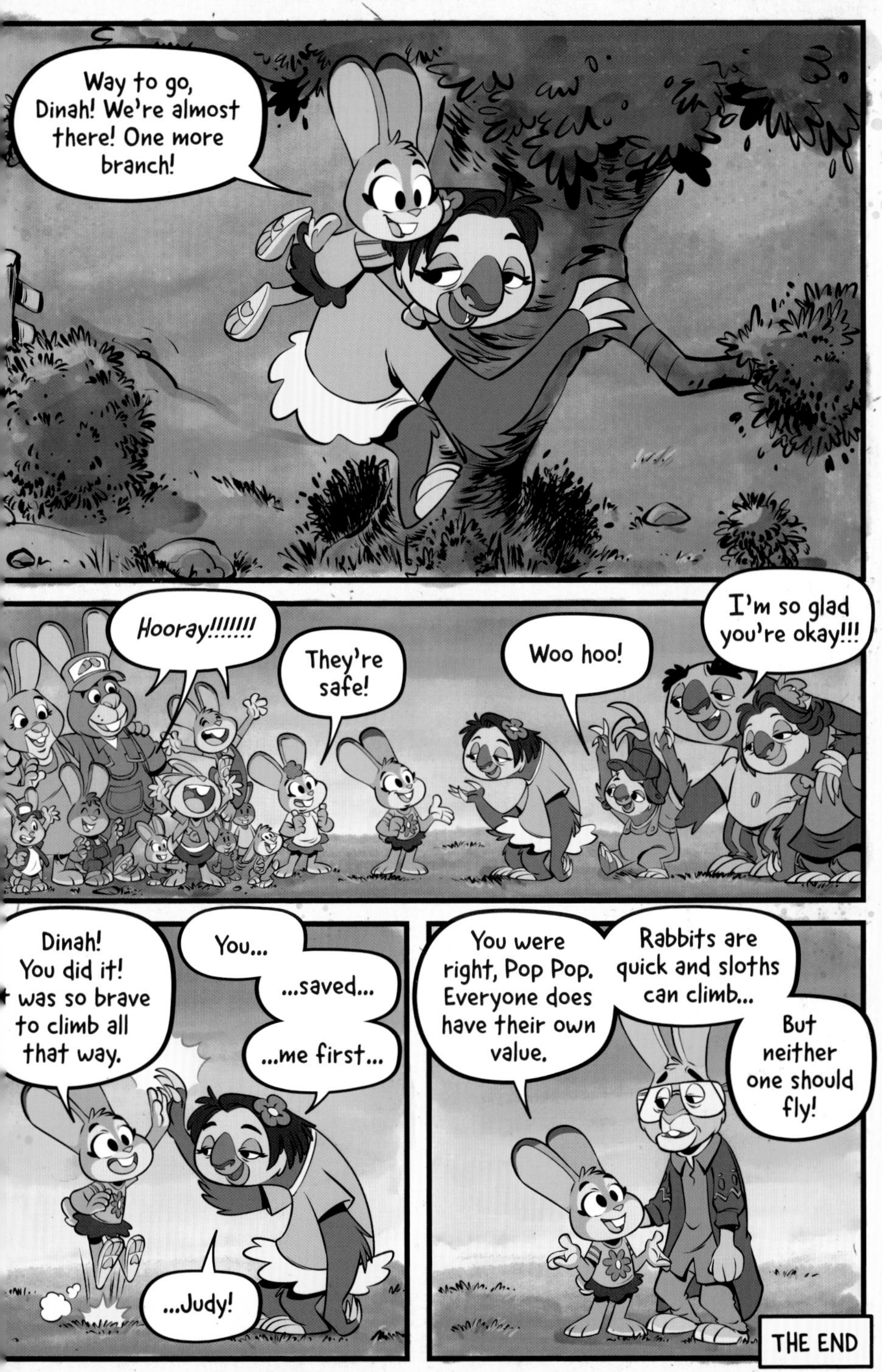
Way to go, Dinah! We're almost there! One more branch!
Hooray!!!!!!!
They're safe!
Woo hoo!
I'm so glad you're okay!!!
Dinah! You did it! [It] was so brave to climb all that way.
You...
...saved...
...me first...
...Judy!
You were right, Pop Pop. Everyone does have their own value.
Rabbits are quick and sloths can climb...
But neither one should fly!
THE END

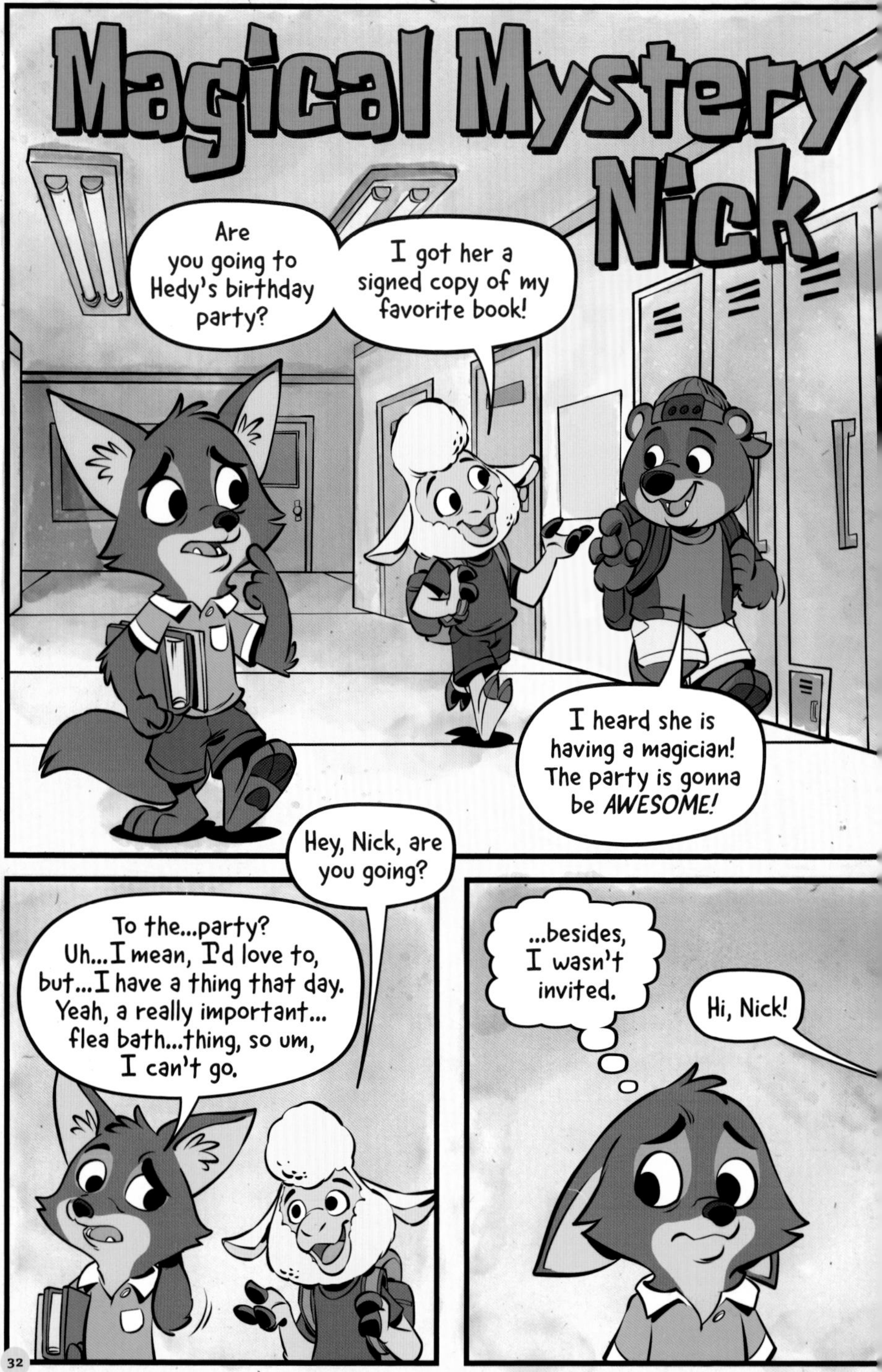

Magical Mystery Nick
Are you going to Hedy's birthday party?
I got her a signed copy of my favorite book!
I heard she is having a magician! The party is gonna be AWESOME!
Hey, Nick, are you going?
To the...party? Uh...I mean, I'd love to, but...I have a thing that day. Yeah, a really important... flea bath...thing, so um, I can't go.
...besides, I wasn't invited.
Hi, Nick!

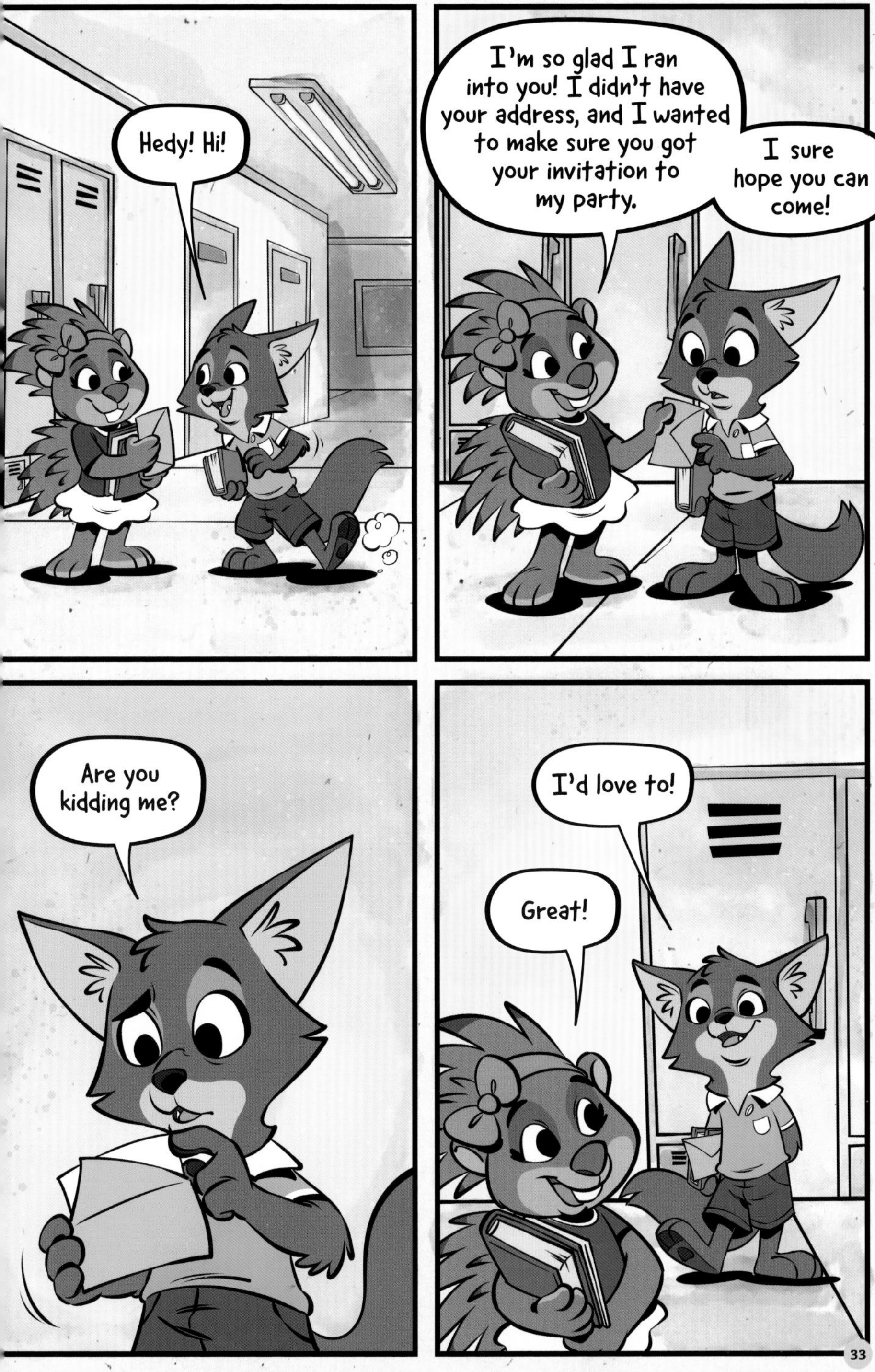
Hedy! Hi!
I'm so glad I ran into you! I didn't have your address, and I wanted to make sure you got your invitation to my party.
I sure hope you can come!
Are you kidding me?
I'd love to!
Great!

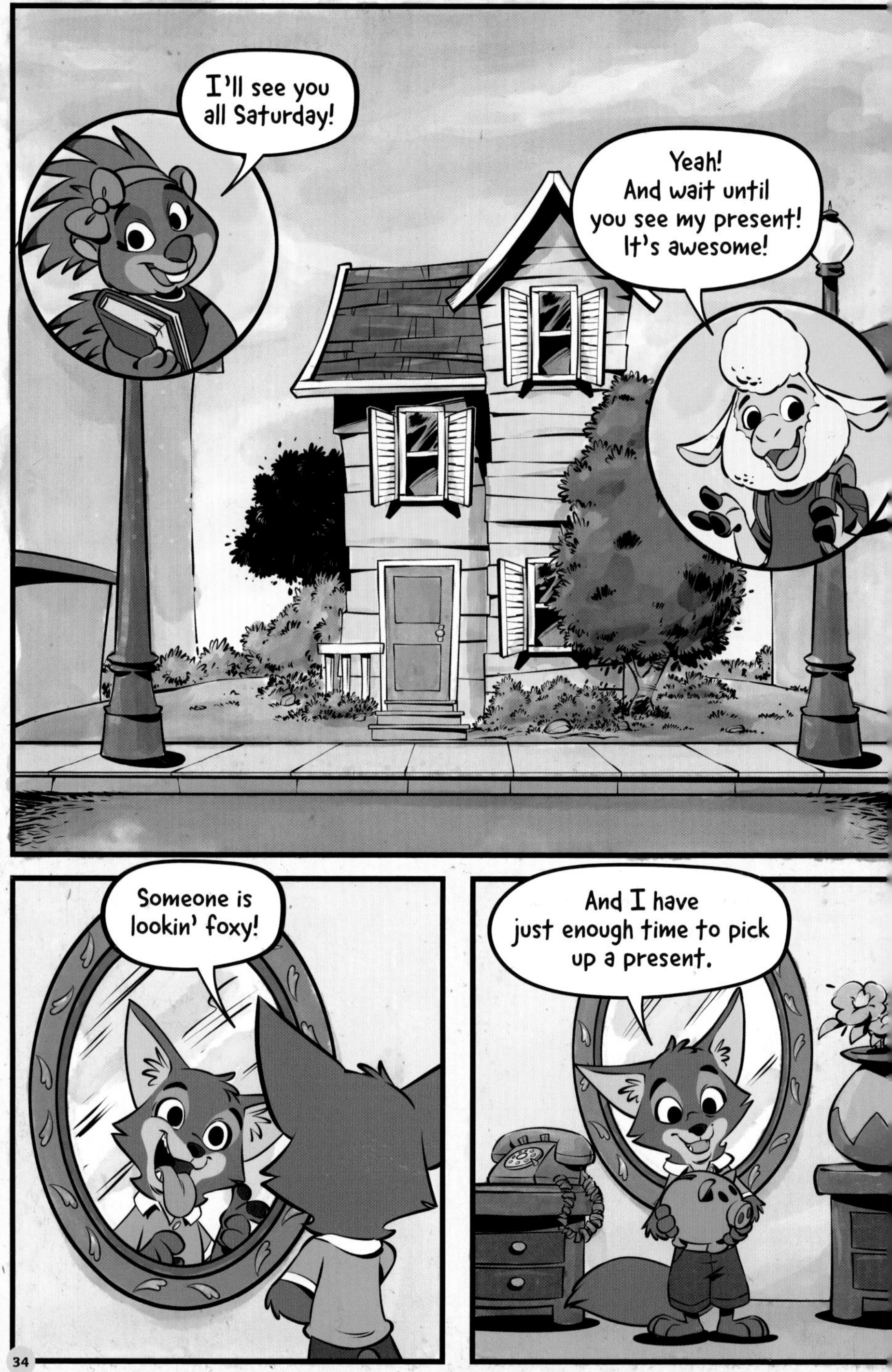
I'll see you all Saturday!
Yeah! And wait until you see my present! It's awesome!
Someone is lookin' foxy!
And I have just enough time to pick up a present.

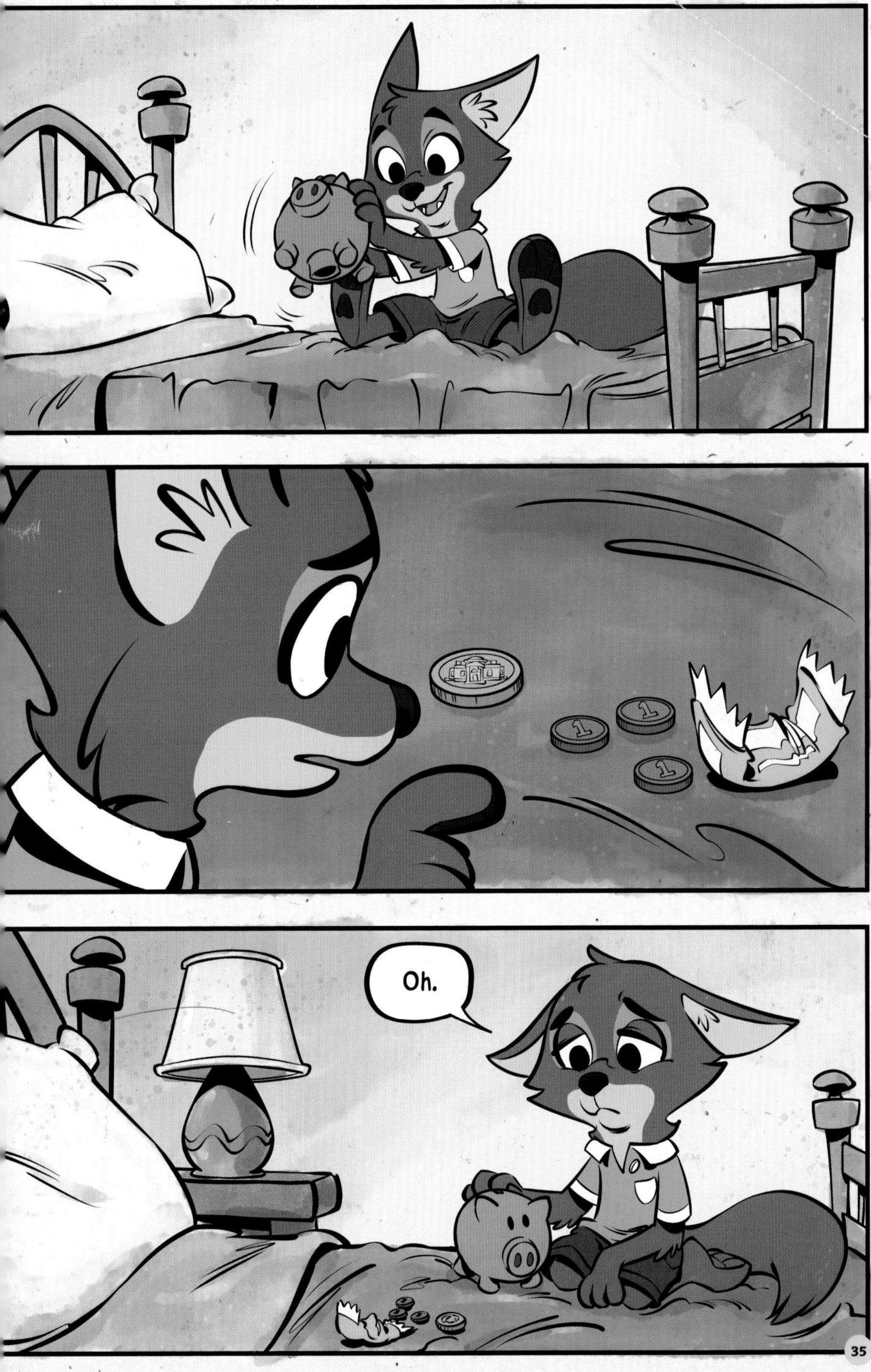

Oh.

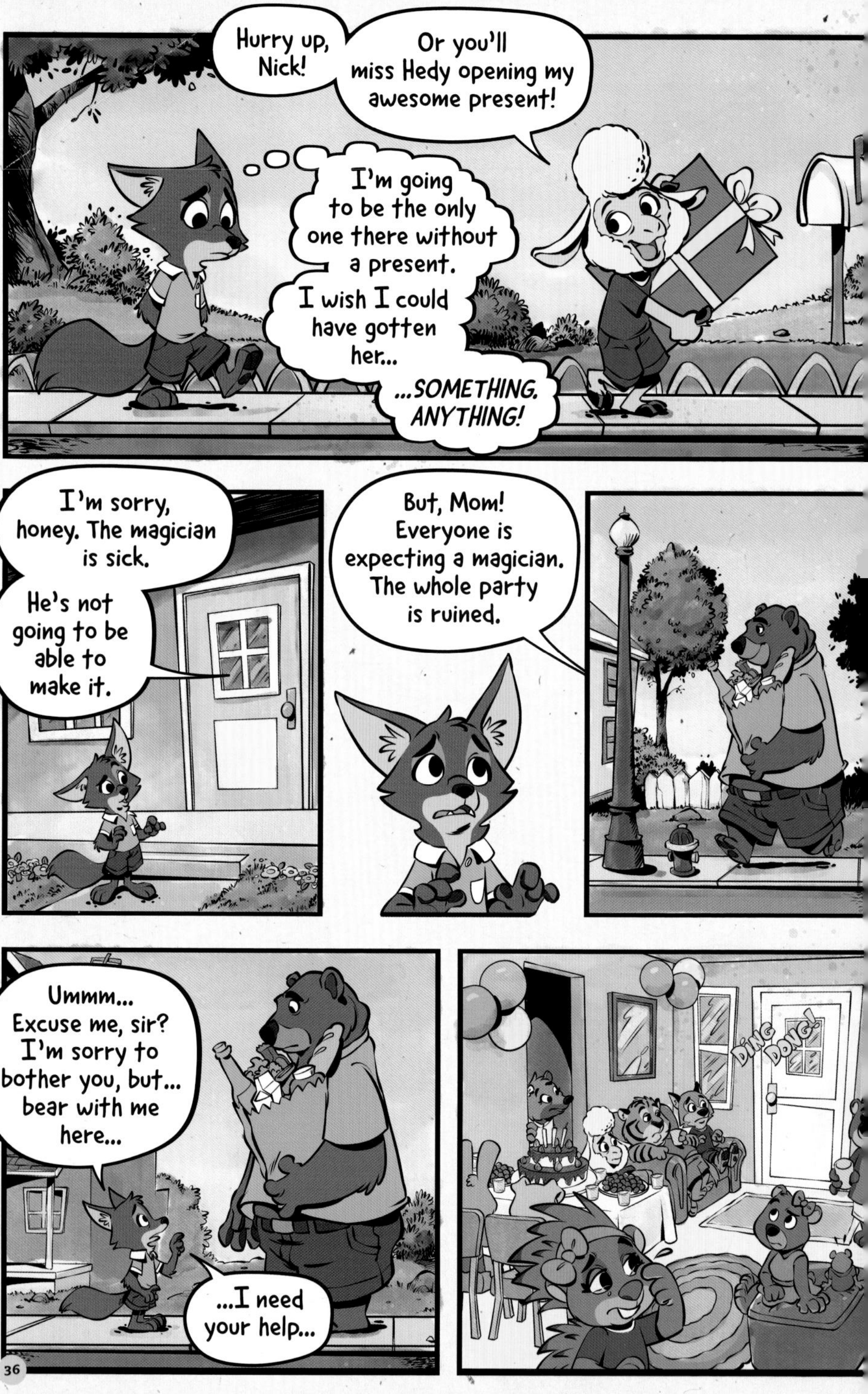
Hurry up, Nick!
Or you'll miss Hedy opening my awesome present!
I'm going to be the only one there without a present.
I wish I could have gotten her...
...SOMETHING. ANYTHING!
I'm sorry, honey. The magician is sick.
He's not going to be able to make it.
But, Mom! Everyone is expecting a magician. The whole party is ruined.
Ummm... Excuse me, sir? I'm sorry to bother you, but... bear with me here...
...I need your help...
DING DONG!

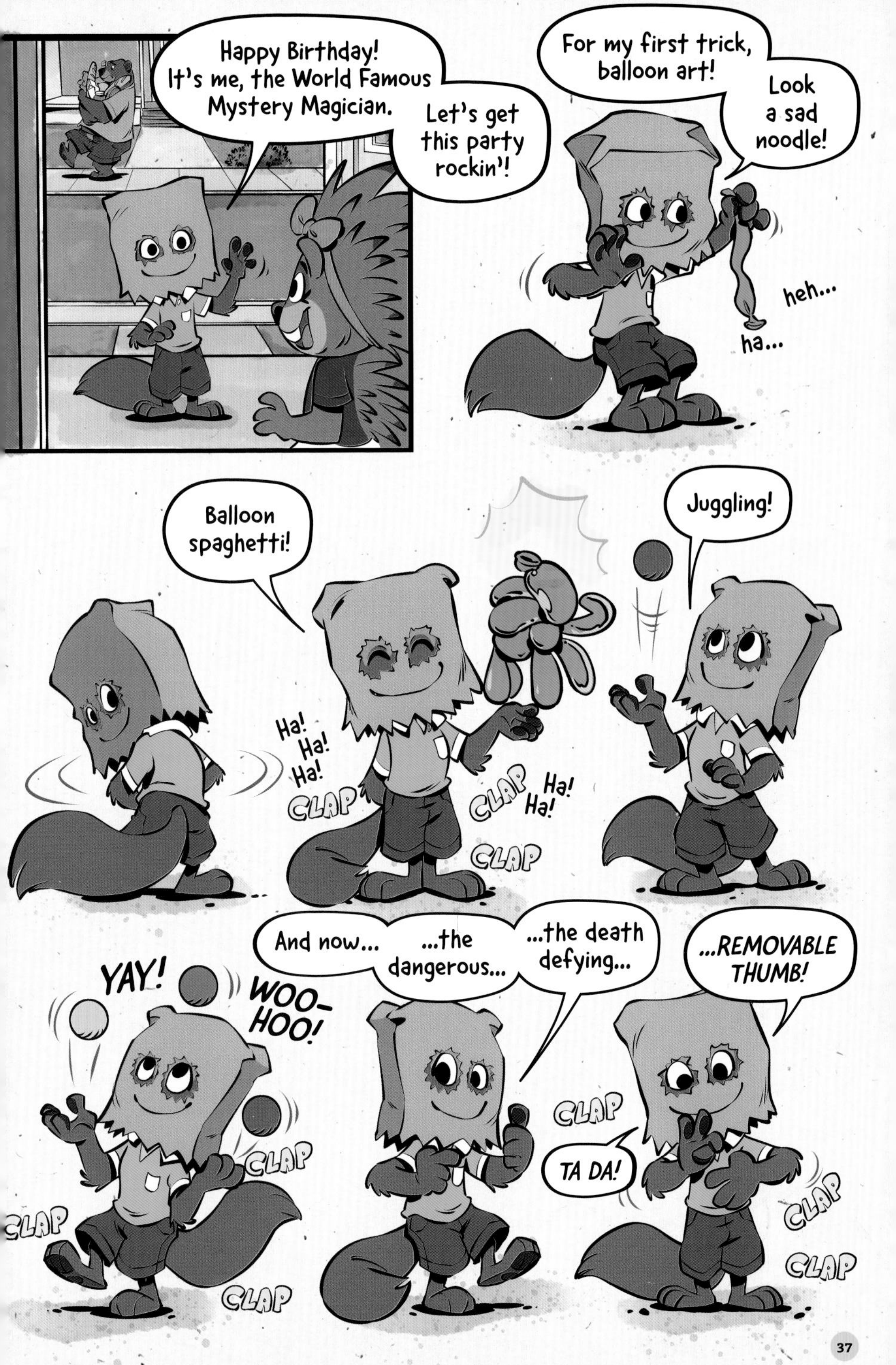
Happy Birthday! It's me, the World Famous Mystery Magician.
Let's get this party rockin'!
For my first trick, balloon art!
Look a sad noodle!
heh...
ha...
Balloon spaghetti!
Ha! Ha! Ha!
CLAP
CLAP
Ha! Ha!
CLAP
Juggling!
YAY!
WOO-HOO!
CLAP
CLAP
CLAP
And now...
...the dangerous...
...the death defying...
...REMOVABLE THUMB!
CLAP
TA DA!
CLAP
CLAP

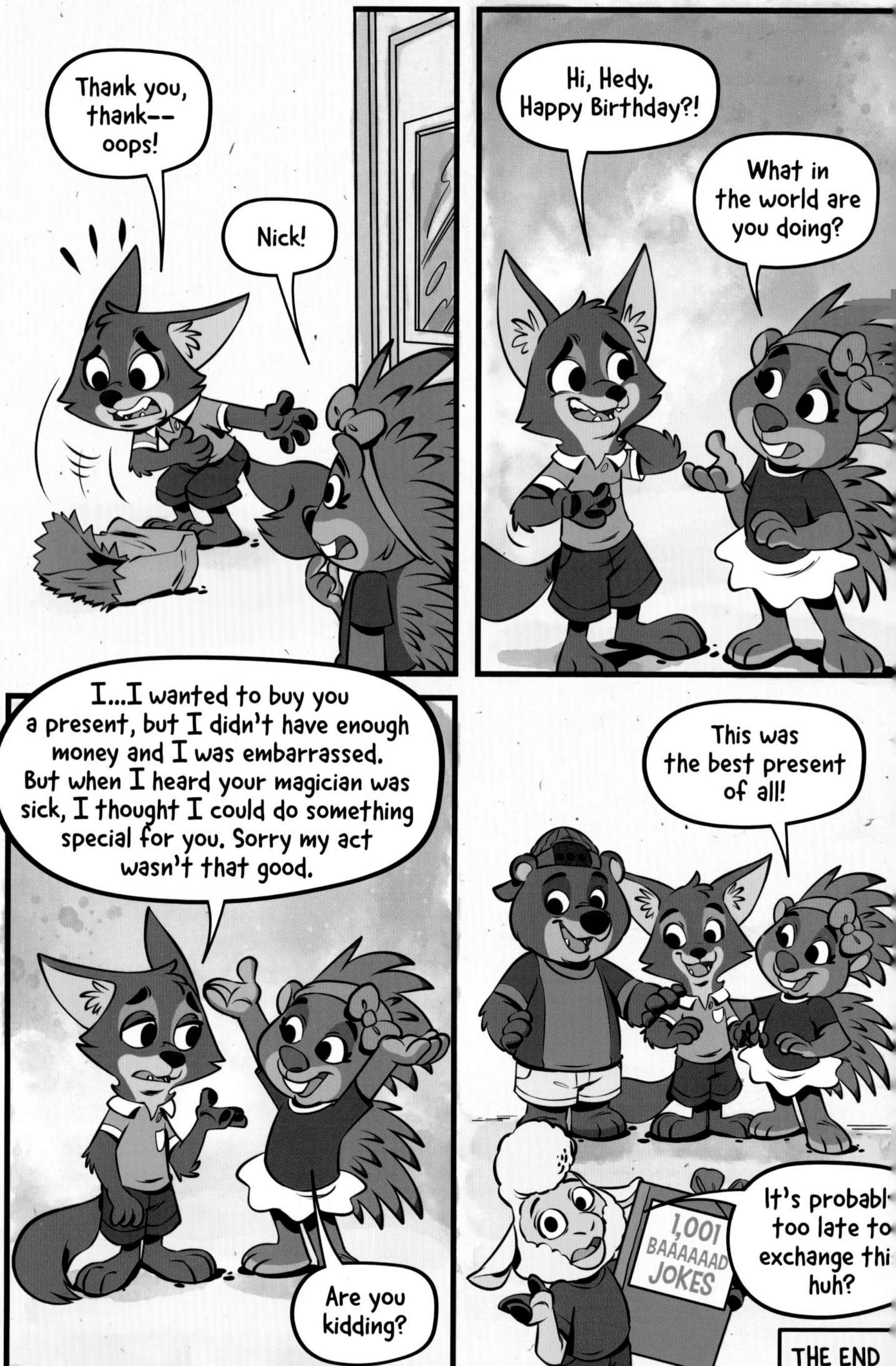

Thank you, thank-- oops!
Nick!
Hi, Hedy. Happy Birthday?!
What in the world are you doing?
I...I wanted to buy you a present, but I didn't have enough money and I was embarrassed. But when I heard your magician was sick, I thought I could do something special for you. Sorry my act wasn't that good.
Are you kidding?
This was the best present of all!
1,001 BAAAAAAD JOKES
It's probabl too late to exchange thi huh?
THE END

A MENAGERIE OF ACTIVITIES FOR MEGA-FUN!

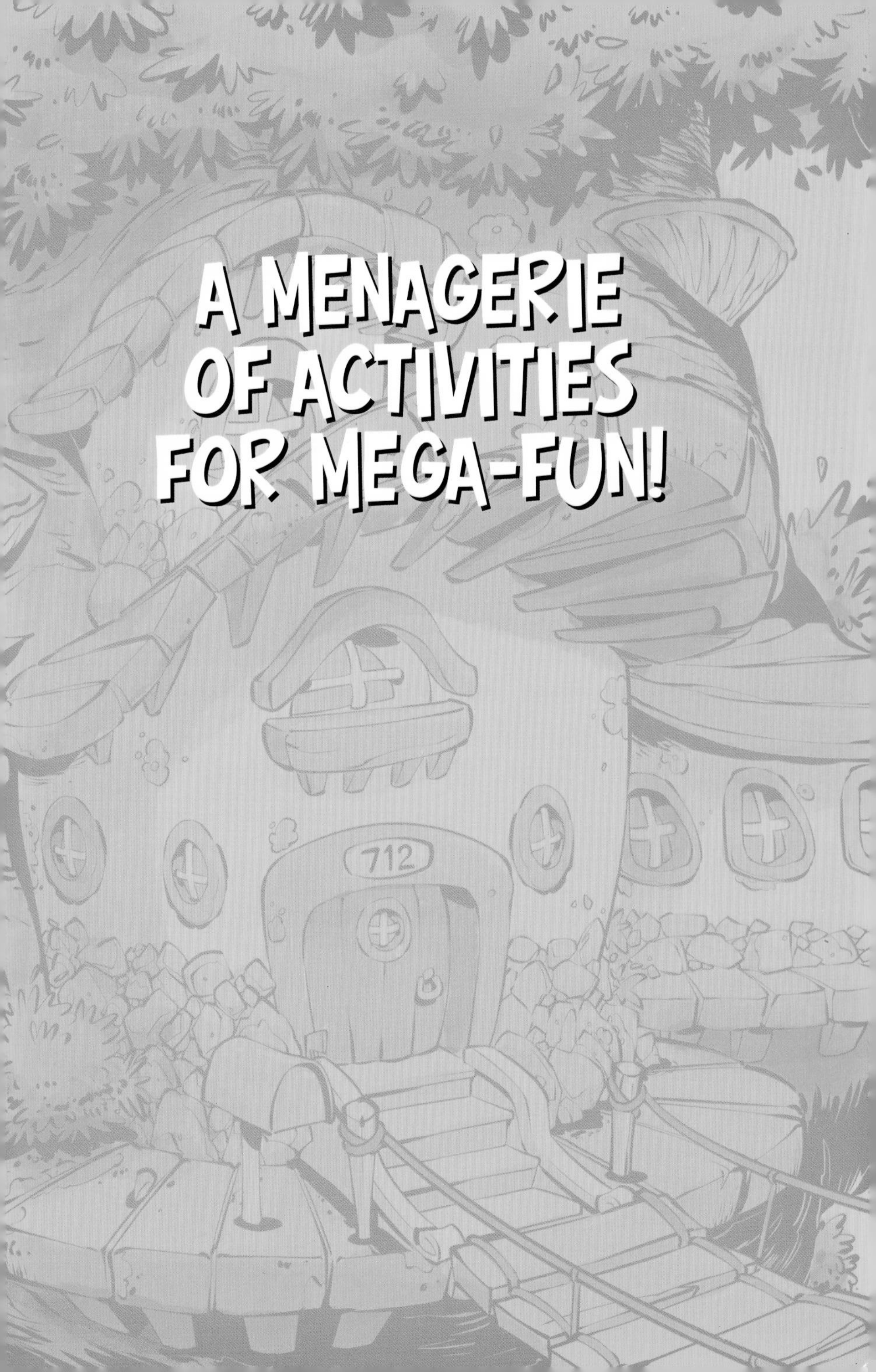
712

WHAT'S MISSING

LOOK AT THE TWO PICTURES ON THESE PAGES OF JUDY AND HER BROTHERS AND SISTERS HELPING THEIR MOM IN THE KITCHEN. IT'S THE SAME PICTURE . . . OR IS IT? CAN YOU SPOT 10 DIFFERENCES BETWEEN PICTURE A, AND PICTURE B? THERE ARE SOME THINGS MISSING!

A

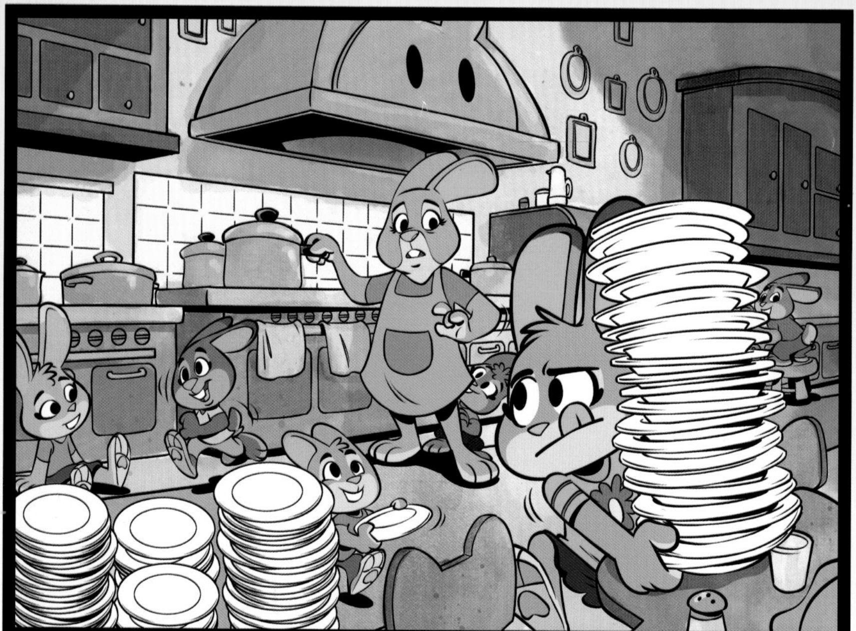

OM THE PICTURE?

WHEN YOU THINK YOU'VE FOUND ALL THE DIFFERENCES YOU CAN CHECK YOUR ANSWERS AT THE BOTTOM OF PAGE 43!

B

SCAVENGER HUNT!

CAN YOU FIND THESE ITEMS IN THE "JUDY IN THE SKY WITH DINAH" STORY?

❶ remote control

❷ light bulb

❸ knife and fork

❹ brown mouse

❺ red truck

CAN YOU FIND THESE ITEMS IN THE "MAGICAL MYSTERY NICK" STORY?

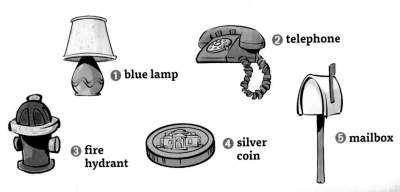

❶ blue lamp

❷ telephone

❸ fire hydrant

❹ silver coin

❺ mailbox

Scavenger Hunt answer key:
"Magical Mystery Nick": blue lamp, page 35; telephone, page 35; fire hydrant, page 36; silver coin, page 35; mailbox, page 36

Scavenger Hunt answer key:
"Judy in the Sky with Dinah": remote control, page 19; light bulb, page 30; knife and fork, page 13; brown mouse, page 7; red truck, page 20

TELL ME A STORY . . .

CHOOSE ONE CHARACTER, ONE OBJECT, ONE LOCATION, AND ONE PROBLEM OR TASK FROM THE FOUR BOXES BELOW. THEN WITH ALL THOSE CHOSEN ITEMS, WRITE OR DRAW A STORY!

PICK A CHARACTER
- Judy
- Dinah
- Judy's mom
- Judy's sister

PICK A PROBLEM OR TASK
- missed the bus
- makes a friend
- is lost
- joins a new club

PICK AN OBJECT
- a backpack
- a dozen carrots
- a book
- broken dishes

PICK A LOCATION
- at a farm
- at school
- at the county fair
- at Judy's house

Once you've created one story, make another one—but try choosing completely different items. Or, for an *extra* challenge, have *someone else* choose the four items for you to use in your story!

What's Missing from the Picture answer key:

43

WHAT'S MISSING

LOOK AT THE TWO PICTURES ON THESE PAGES OF HEDY'S BIRTHDAY PARTY. IT'S THE SAME PICTURE . . . OR IS IT? CAN YOU SPOT 10 DIFFERENCES BETWEEN PICTURE A, AND PICTURE B? THERE ARE SOME THINGS MISSING!

A

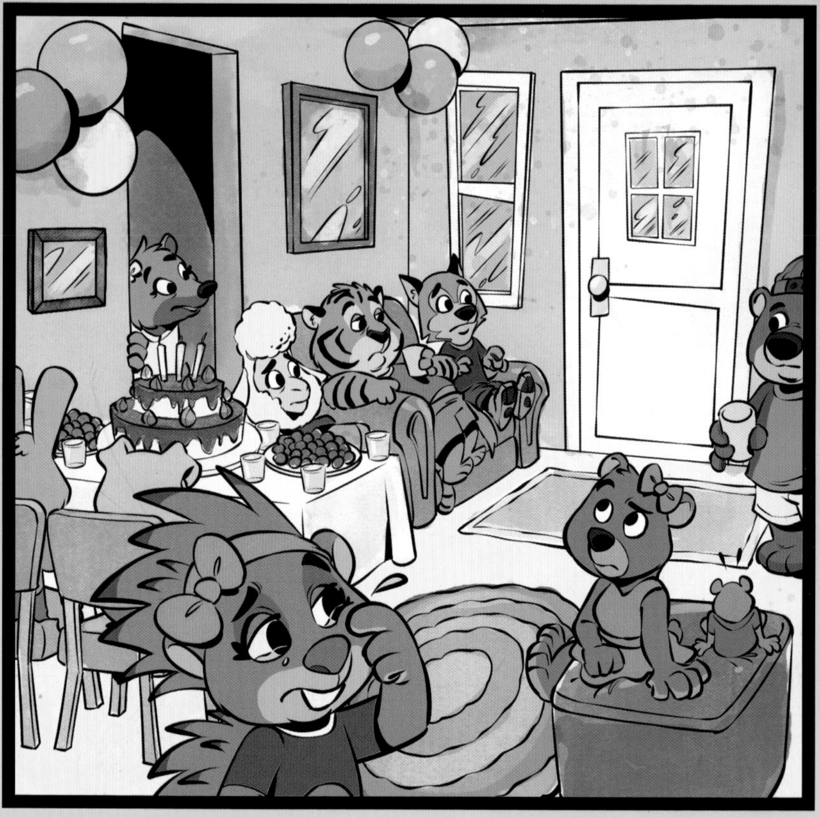

OM THE PICTURE?

WHEN YOU THINK YOU'VE FOUND ALL THE
DIFFERENCES YOU CAN CHECK YOUR ANSWERS
AT THE BOTTOM OF PAGE 46!

B

WHO AM I?

For this activity, you'll need a partner!

IMAGINE YOURSELF AS ONE OF THE FOUR CHARACTERS FROM THE "MAGICAL MYSTERY NICK" STORY, SHOWN BELOW—BUT KEEP IT A SECRET FROM YOUR PARTNER BECAUSE THEY ARE GOING TO TRY TO GUESS WHO YOU ARE!

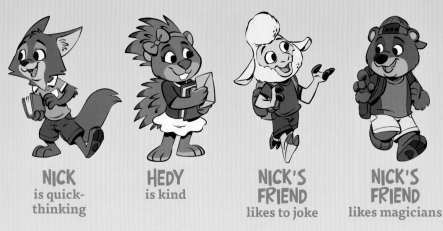

NICK
is quick-thinking

HEDY
is kind

NICK'S FRIEND
likes to joke

NICK'S FRIEND
likes magicians

Once you've decided who you are going to be, your partner can start asking you questions about yourself, until they can guess who you are. But, here's the hard part: you can only answer questions with "yes," "no," or "I don't know." **Below are a few examples of questions your partner might ask you!**

- Do you like to eat fruits and vegetables?
- Do you have fur? • Do you have paws?
- Are you wearing something on your head?
- Is your shirt red?

Once your partner has successfully guessed who you are, swap roles! Have your partner pick one of the characters and *you* ask the questions.

For an extra challenge, try this activity with a different character from Nick's story—there are lots of other kids at Hedy's birthday party!

What's Missing from the Picture answer key:

DARK HORSE BOOKS

president and publisher Mike Richardson • collection editor Freddye Miller • collection assistant editors Jenny Blenk, Judy Khuu • collection designer David Nestelle • digital art technician Christianne Gillenardo-Goudreau

Neil Hankerson Executive Vice President • Tom Weddle Chief Financial Officer • Randy Stradley Vice President of Publishing • Nick McWhorter Chief Business Development Officer • Matt Parkinson Vice President of Marketing • Dale LaFountain Vice President of Information Technology • Cara Niece Vice President of Production and Scheduling • Mark Bernardi Vice President of Book Trade and Digital Sales • Ken Lizzi General Counsel • Dave Marshall Editor in Chief • Davey Estrada Editorial Director • Chris Warner Senior Books Editor • Cary Grazzini Director of Specialty Projects • Lia Ribacchi Art Director • Vanessa Todd-Holmes Director of Print Purchasing • Matt Dryer Director of Digital Art and Prepress • Michael Gombos Director of International Publishing and Licensing • Kari Yadro Director of Custom Programs

DISNEY PUBLISHING WORLDWIDE GLOBAL MAGAZINES, COMICS AND PARTWORKS

Publisher Lynn Waggoner • EDITORIAL TEAM Bianca Coletti (Director, Magazines), Guido Frazzini (Director, Comics), Carlotta Quattrocolo (Executive Editor), Stefano Ambrosio (Executive Editor, New IP), Camilla Vedove (Senior Manager, Editorial Development), Behnoosh Khalili (Senior Editor), Julie Dorris (Senior Editor), Mina Riazi (Assistant Editor), Jonathan Manning (Assistant Editor) • DESIGN Enrico Soave (Senior Designer) • ART Ken Shue (VP, Global Art), Manny Mederos (Senior Illustration Manager, Comics and Magazines), Roberto Santillo (Creative Director), Marco Ghiglione (Creative Manager), Stefano Attardi (Computer Art Designer) • PORTFOLIO MANAGEMENT Olivia Ciancarelli (Director) • BUSINESS & MARKETING Mariantonietta Galla (Marketing Manager), Virpi Korhonen (Editorial Manager)

Zootopia: Friends to the Rescue

Published by Dark Horse Books
A division of Dark Horse Comics, Inc.
10956 SE Main Street
Milwaukie, OR 97222

DarkHorse.com

To find a comics shop in your area, visit comicshoplocator.com

First edition: September 2018
ISBN 978-1-50671-054-9

1 3 5 7 9 10 8 6 4 2
Printed in China

AW YEAH COMICS!
Art Baltazar, Franco, and more!
It's up to Action Cat and Adventure Bug to stop the
bad guys! Follow these amazing superheroes created
by Art Baltazar and Franco in this comic extravaganza
with bonus stories from the Aw Yeah bullpen!

Volume 1: And . . . Action!
ISBN 978-1-61655-558-0
Volume 2: Time for . . . Adventure!
ISBN 978-1-61655-689-1
Volume 3: Make Way . . . for Awesome!
ISBN 978-1-50670-045-8
Action Cat & Adventure Bug
ISBN 978-1-50670-023-6
$12.99 each

BIRD BOY
Anne Szabla
Bali, a ten-year-old boy, is desperate to prove his worth
to his northern tribe despite his small stature. Banned
from the ceremony that would make him an adult in the
eyes of his people, he takes matters into his own hands.
To prove that he is capable of taking care of himself, he
sets out into the forbidden forest and stumbles upon a
legendary weapon.

Volume 1: The Sword of Mali Mani
ISBN 978-1-61655-930-4
Volume 2: The Liminal Wood
ISBN 978-1-61655-968-7
$9.99 each

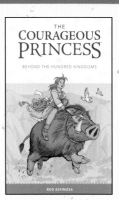

THE COURAGEOUS PRINCESS
Rod Espinosa
Once upon a time, a greedy dragon kidnapped
a beloved princess . . . But if you think she
just waited around for some charming prince
to rescue her, then you're in for a surprise!
Princess Mabelrose has enough brains and
bravery to fend for herself!

Volume 1: Beyond the Hundred Kingdoms
ISBN 978-1-61655-722-5
Volume 2: The Unremembered Lands
ISBN 978-1-61655-723-2
Volume 3: The Dragon Queen
ISBN 978-1-61655-724-9
$19.99 each

ITTY BITTY COMICS
Art Baltazar, Franco
Follow the adventures of your favorite Dark Horse
heroes—now pintsized!

Itty Bitty Hellboy ISBN 978-1-61655-414-9 **$9.99**
Itty Bitty Hellboy: The Search for the Were-Jaguar!
ISBN 978-1-61655-801-7 **$12.99**
Itty Bitty Mask ISBN 978-1-61655-683-9 **$12.99**

GLISTER
Andi Watson
Strange things happen around Glister Butterworth.
A young girl living on her family's English estate,
Glister has unusual adventures every day, like the
arrival of a teapot haunted by a demanding ghost, a
crop of new relatives blooming on the family tree, a
stubborn house that walks off its land in a huff, and
a trip to Faerieland to find her missing mother.

ISBN 978-1-50670-319-0 **$14.99**

SCARY GODMOTHER
Jill Thompson
It's Halloween night and it's up to Scary Godmother
to show one little girl just how much fun spooky can
be! Hannah Marie with the help of Scary Godmother
will stand up to her mean-spirited cousin Jimmy
and her fear of monsters on her first Halloween
adventure with the big kids.

ISBN 978-1-59582-589-6
Comic Book Stories ISBN 978-1-59582-723-4
$24.99 each

DARKHORSE.COM

AVAILABLE AT YOUR LOCAL COMICS SHOP OR BOOKSTORE | TO FIND A COMICS SHOP IN YOUR AREA, VISIT COMICSHOPLOCATOR.COM

For more information or to order direct: On the web: DarkHorse.com •Email: mailorder@darkhorse.com •Phone: 1-800-862-0052 Mon.–Fri. 9 AM to 5 PM Pacific Time.

Aw Yeah Comics™ © Arthur Baltazar and Franco Aureliani. Hellboy™ © Mike Mignola. The Mask® © Dark Horse Comics, Inc. The Courageous Princess™ © Rod Espinosa. Bird Boy™ © Anne Szabla.
Glister™ © Andrew Watson. Scary Godmother™ © Jill Thompson. Dark Horse Books® and the Dark Horse logo are registered trademarks of Dark Horse Comics, Inc. All rights reserved. (BL 6002 P2)